DO WHAT THEY SAY OR ELSE

ANNIE ERNAUX

Do What They Say or Else

TRANSLATED BY

Christopher Beach
and Carrie Noland

UNIVERSITY OF NEBRASKA PRESS   LINCOLN

First published in French as *Ce qu'ils disent ou rien*.
© Editions Gallimard 1977. Translation © 2022 by
the Board of Regents of the University of Nebraska.

The University of Nebraska Press is part of a land-
grant institution with campuses and programs on the
past, present, and future homelands of the Pawnee,
Ponca, Otoe-Missouria, Omaha, Dakota, Lakota,
Kaw, Cheyenne, and Arapaho Peoples, as well as
those of the relocated Ho-Chunk, Sac and Fox, and
Iowa Peoples.

Publication of this volume was assisted by the
International Center for Writing and Translation at
the University of California, Irvine.

Library of Congress Cataloging-in-Publication Data
Names: Ernaux, Annie, 1940– author. | Beach,
Christopher, 1959– translator. | Noland, Carrie,
1958– translator.
Title: Do what they say or else / Annie Ernaux;
translated by Christopher Beach and Carrie Noland.
Other titles: Ce qu'ils disent ou rien. English
Description: Lincoln: University
of Nebraska Press, [2022]
Identifiers: LCCN 2022008358
ISBN 9781496228000 (paperback)
ISBN 9781496232755 (epub)
ISBN 9781496232762 (pdf)
Subjects: BISAC: FICTION / Coming of Age |
FICTION / World Literature / France /
20th Century | LCGFT: Novels.
Classification: LCC PQ2665.R67 C413 2022 |
DDC 843/.914—dc23/eng/20220307
LC record available at
https://lccn.loc.gov/2022008358

Designed and set in Linotype Janson by N. Putens.

DO WHAT THEY SAY OR ELSE

SOMETIMES I HAVE THE FEELING THAT I HAVE SECRETS. They aren't really secrets, because I don't want to talk about them, and besides, they're things that can't be told to anyone. They're too strange. Céline is going out with a guy from our high school, a junior. He's waiting to meet her at four o'clock on the corner next to the post office. At least it's clear what *her* secret is. If I was her I wouldn't even hide it. But the person who I am has no shape. Just thinking about it makes me feel heavy, like a real fatso. I'd like to sleep until a time when I could understand myself better—maybe when I'm eighteen or twenty-one. There must come a day when everything is clear, when everything falls into place. From then on, there's nothing to do but walk the straight and narrow, married with two children and a job that isn't too pitiful. There was a theme for a paper: "Talk about your dreams for the future." I got a good grade on it. The future. When I see all those years of reading books stretching out in front of me, I feel like I have a hole in my head. There are all these things that I don't know yet and that I will have to be able to write and say. When I was little I would slide down, on purpose, all the way to the bottom of the bed. I didn't want to get up, and it was dark and warm there. I feel the same way now. Last year I was only thinking about starting high school.

Of course, the teachers were trying to scare us: "Your grades are just barely good enough . . ." They acted calm and dignified, but that didn't help us much when it came to getting onto the academic track in high school. "You just have to be more intelligent. It's not our fault if you don't make it." At home, my mother was always bitching: "You only got an 8 out of 20 in math! That's not good. If you just put in a little effort, you'd do better. Do you want to end up working in a factory?" I know she's right, and there's nothing I can say back. If I didn't go to high school—wham!—I would have to start working. Even so, when she was nagging me, around the time of the high school orientation last March, I didn't like it. It would have been better if she hadn't said anything. Now she's feeling reassured. There won't be any more fuss until the exam for the *bac*. I didn't tell her that at the end of the first year you could be kicked out of high school or switched to a technical track. She would've made a big deal about it all year long. My parents don't have their high school diplomas, and yet they're a thousand times more annoying about it than Céline's parents, who are engineers or something. It's true that her parents don't need to yell at her. They're the living example of success, whereas in the case of my parents, who are manual workers, I have to be what they tell me to be and not what they are. I don't know if I'll be able to become a schoolteacher, or even if I still want to be one now. My father irritates me. He's always watching me anxiously. "Doesn't it hurt your brain to have your face in a book all the time?" Reading's not his strong suit: he only reads the newspaper: *Paris-Normandie*, and once in a while *France-Soir*. Sometimes, when he isn't paying attention, his lips move while he reads. Maybe he's right: my classes *are* too hard. At the beginning of the school year, I believed that when I was in school I would only think about studying. The only people I knew in my grade were Céline and one inoffensive little fourteen-year-old boy. And no, I don't have any more ideas for French compositions. The teacher criticizes me for being disorganized. On my first assignment she wrote, "The topic was good, but you didn't do this and that with it." Fine, it's settled: I'll never know how to treat the topic in the right way. That's the problem. It's impossible to catch up, or to change anything about yourself. If only that was true just for French composition. I can see myself plummeting, and I don't even know what to call what I'm feeling. What good would it do to say I'm in love, since I'll never see him again and all boys disgust me? Sometimes I feel afraid, not so much about having to work in a factory—my parents push that one too far, since I would always be able to find an office job—but of never wanting anything again, and of being the only one like me. "You're not like other girls. We have to pull the words out of your mouth. There are so many other girls who are so nice, girls who would know how to appreciate what we do for you." They're always making comparisons, but never with the same girls. Why are other girls so clear-cut? Céline, when she gets up in front of me in math class, barely moves her back: there's just a harmonious movement of her ass. Has she done it yet? I feel like a bug next to her, flat-chested, with no big tits like she has. What do I look like? I wish I was still back in June, at the end of middle school. It was terribly hot. My father was saying that according to the television news we would need rain soon for people's gardens. Yesterday I saw myself in the window of the shoe store. It was raining cats and dogs, and I had strands of hair hanging down everywhere. Summer vacation is definitely over. I look ugly with my glasses on. I don't take them off anymore, since they leave little marks on either side of my nose, which I touch when I'm really bored in class. I don't care about those marks now. My mother watches me leave for school, saying casually, "You look good with your glasses on, really good. They make you look serious." People in my family say I look like a schoolteacher. At least I already have the glasses for it. I started taking them off in June, near the end of the school year. I had trouble at first, since I couldn't distinguish people I passed on the sidewalk anymore. They seemed to be walking in a foggy light, as if they were on a badly adjusted color television. The problem was that I couldn't say hello because I wasn't completely sure who it was. I didn't want to be taken for an idiot when I got the face wrong. It was also bothersome not to recognize people from my personal orbit. What a scene there would be at home if I didn't say hello to a teacher, or to someone I should know by sight, like one of the neighbors. At what age do you start saying hello to people without thinking about it? It was even worse in elementary school. I got so worried about it that I would cross to the other side of the street. The woman who owns the tree nursery, Madame Bachelot, wouldn't look at me from behind her fence. She stood there stiff as a poker. When I would say "Hello, ma'am," she didn't answer, and then afterward she would look me over from every angle. She really hurt my feelings, the old hag, and she told my mother that I stepped down off the sidewalk just before her house. "Who does your little girl think she is?" I got in a lot of trouble. The Bachelots were a big deal, worth millions, though they weren't stuck up. My parents almost think it's all right for them to have a lot of money, since they don't act like it. Not being able to see people was fine with me. I would put nothing on under my dress, which has shoulder straps and is tight-fitting at the top and low-cut. If I walked too fast, the fabric would bunch up between my legs and get tugged into my behind, which showed everything. "You always want things that aren't made for you. For the same price, you could have gotten something youthful, something more suitable for a young girl.

You're just calling attention to yourself." She had let me choose it, but then she got mad about it. It's true that I was a bit ashamed to wear it, but I felt like I was forced to show myself off in it. You can't stay a kid forever. I would go for walks wearing just the dress, with my glasses in my bag. If I happened to run into my mother or my father, I could always say that I got dirt on the lenses, and that's why I took them off. You have to prepare your defense. Wearing the dress gave me a funny feeling. I felt like I was presenting a new collection, like in *Jours de France* magazine, to an audience I saw as a blur. Sweat was sticking to the tops of my legs, and it was difficult to walk naturally when I passed by the outdoor terraces of cafés on the post office square. And then, when I arrived at school, there were those first ten meters inside the courtyard. The boys, and the girls too, were watching to see if I really had a bust. I didn't lower my eyes too much. You might have thought I was stuck up. I took my time putting on my blouse before going upstairs to my classroom. I never would have dared to do that the year before, since I didn't have enough of a bust. But last year there was the middle school diploma exam. It was as if having a problem to solve authorized me to go for it. I've always felt that you can't be afraid of two things at the same time. The stronger fear will always tilt the scales, and in that case it was the exam. Also, everything was starting to get crazy at school. They were still keeping track of absences, but not for any apparent reason. The teachers didn't seem too clever, carefully noting down the names of students who had already taken off. It seemed to me that they lowered their standards when June came around. Their threats no longer served any purpose, and even the middle school diploma exam was no longer under their control. They would be as surprised as we were by what questions would be on it. The following year, they would repeat the things that we now knew to other students. They could make the students sweat for one year—two years at the most—and then, "No way, José, we're out of here!" We were moving on, and they weren't. I leafed through the textbooks, looking at math problems that I would never do, some of which had thrown me for a loop at the beginning of the school year. They no longer had any power over me. I felt that I had grown a bit older. Because of the heat, we studied under the lime trees in the courtyard. I would have liked to see that month of June go on for longer. It was the first time I'd been able to think so clearly. I was happy. It's too bad there was the exam and all the studying: otherwise, I could have paid more attention to everything that was happening to me and taken full advantage of it. The prospect of the exam held me back a bit. I told myself that if I failed it I'd be willing to do anything. I would sleep with a boy, whatever the cost. I had always been afraid that I would die before I got to experience that. There was no point in living up to then—having gone through my whole boring childhood, and having thought about it all the time—and all for nothing. Besides, if I had to die, in a war for example, I would throw myself at the first guy who came along. It could have been a friend, or even François the hall monitor. In the case of a war, I definitely would have done it with him, but he wouldn't have been able to keep up with demand, and there are prettier girls than me. The heat was giving me dirty ideas that I wouldn't have dared to share with the others but that I wasn't ashamed of because it was nearly the end of middle school. Leaving a place gives you more freedom in the way you think. I'd never noticed the bodies of my girlfriends so much before. Not in the winter, for sure, with everything you have on. I was comparing them with me: their weight, their butts, their legs, their hair. How did my body stack up? I was about Odile's height, I was a brunette like Céline, and, as for breasts, it's difficult to know for sure with bras on. What would I rather have, good grades or a good body? It would be too much to ask for both. We can't expect to get everything in life. If your body develops too quickly, it must be a drain on the intelligence. Even the teachers are wary of the girls who are too good-looking. In June, Céline cut her hair in a bob. I saw her moist neck as she stood, leaning against a wall, her legs spread apart. It bothered me to see her like that, with her jeans stretched tight against just the right spot. She made me think about a day in the house we had lived in before, on Rue Césarine. In the toolshed, there was her laugh and her small, wide-spaced eyes, as she sat on an overturned crate. And there was her "that thing," as we privately called it, which I had discovered was as different from mine as her laugh was, or her thighs that were covered in little goosebumps. I had come to understand my own mystery of something soft and pink. It looked like the inside of the beaks of the hens that my grandmother forced open with scissors to kill. Her first pubic hairs had already come, and I wondered when I would have them. "Swear that you'll show me a sanitary pad full of blood!" But all of that was Alberte, not Céline. And now we would not be showing each other our "that thing," or anything else. Even when my Aunt Rose comes to visit, I don't say a word, except "I don't feel like going to the pool today." "Oh, yes, you're 'handicapped.'" But the first time it happened, I wanted the others to know about it. Not the boys, obviously: there was no question of that. At the end of the school year, I was enjoying being with the girls from my class. We tanned ourselves, lying hip to hip, and we smoked behind the lime trees, acting like there was no separation between us. As for what the teachers say, there are students who understand it a bit, or quite a lot, or a whole lot. There are the experts and the not-so-bright. But those weren't the differences that I thought about the most. It had more to do with a way of relaxing, of talking, of indefinable things. There was one small difference between us: the dresses we owned. In June, I only had one new one to wear, and by the time a week had gone by everyone was used to seeing it. "If you pass your exam, I'll buy you another one." I would have preferred to have it right away. Later on, during summer vacation, which is always boring, it wouldn't really matter that much. The vacation also created another slight difference between us, both at the end of the school year and at the beginning of the following year. Céline was going to Yugoslavia for her summer vacation. But we forget about those things afterward and we become equals again. As one girl said: "I wouldn't go to the coast, any coast, not even in Yugoslavia." There were still two years to go before we would finish paying off the house. When I was nearly eight, and it was going to be another ten years before we paid off a three-room house and a yard, it seemed like an eternity of payments. And even then it wouldn't be completely ours. Besides that, it's in a quiet neighborhood where there's nobody around, which is very different from the projects on Rue Césarine where Alberte lives. My father has his vacation in August. We go see the extended family. It's a hundred kilometers at full speed. A Sunday by the seaside, even if it kills them. "You get bored hanging out in town. It's healthy for young people to get out." I must not belong to the "young people" yet. My mother was going to start helping out at the Café de la Petite Vitesse three days a week. She didn't want me to go on vacation by myself, and besides, where would I go? I made a bet with myself that nothing interesting would happen to me during this summer vacation. What bugged me the most is that I wouldn't be able to get rid of the background noise of my parents until September. I had a bad feeling about that. During the school year, you don't see that much of them. You have a thousand ways to forget about their bullshit: classes, talks with your friends, sports. At home, I wouldn't be able to get away from them. In the middle school courtyard, the sixth grade kids barged in on us. I saw myself as I was when I started middle school, and then even before that, when I was in elementary school. There were the same dusty afternoons at the end of the school year, the never-ending recesses, the distant teachers, and images of me as a kid, which disgusted me more and more. I wanted to slap the sixth grade girls when they came over to annoy us. When I was in elementary school, my mother babied me too much. I always carried lots of clothes under my arms to put on, because I had to take off the ones she dressed me in. The big girls pulled me by my free hand. "Come play 'handkerchief' with us." But I didn't know where to put down my bundle of clothes. "Be careful that people don't steal your things." One day I had the handkerchief on my back and I didn't see it. "You're it!" I had to stay in the middle of the circle until the end of the game. I was a pitiful kid, a mommy's girl, the one who got stuck in the middle. Things are actually a bit different when you're nearly sixteen.

On the morning of the exam, my legs were stretched out under the table as I waited for the math section of the test to begin. The teacher was wearing a green top. She was blond. She could have been a salesgirl at Monoprix: I didn't really see any difference. Stupid thoughts were coming into my head at the very moment when they shouldn't be, and then . . . we're off! . . . and I wrote nonstop until the morning session was over. Céline, sitting behind me, was having trouble. Whispering answers to her would have been dangerous, and I didn't really want to anyway. The next day I slept until noon. After that, I spent the whole day wondering how I'd done. Did everything begin there? My parents were eating. My father cut his bread slowly. My mother didn't say anything. I felt like she was angry at me because I made her worry. For all I cared, they might not have existed at all. "You treat us like we don't exist. You don't even tell us how it went. You should at least have some idea how you did!" The fact was, I *didn't* know. They had some nerve! They're not the ones who had to take the test, and yet they pester you about it. The world seemed strange to me. My mother unpeeled her too-hot hard-boiled egg, holding it with a kitchen towel, which she also used as a napkin for meals. She says it's easier that way. The tomatoes, sprinkled with bits of onion, were making me feel sick. My father turned on the one o'clock news: there was a conference in America, inflation was rising again, and the drought continued, as anyone could plainly see. All of that seemed totally insignificant to me. The important thing was what was happening at that moment: the suffocating kitchen, the fridge that had just started running, my hands on the waxed tablecloth, the little knife marks next to my plate. My throat was tight. I wasn't really scared of failing. It was just a stupid middle school exam. But there was something about seeing us at the table and feeling the world around us in a big circle stretching far, far, far away, and yet knowing that everything came back to me. That afternoon I went into town. We always call it that, because there aren't any stores or anything in my neighborhood. "There's not even a place to buy shampoo," I told my mother. With my mother, you always have to have a reason for going out. To help decide my fate, I kept my glasses on, with the thought that if I looked ugly and nerdy I would pass the exam. It's funny: I would've really liked to run into Alberte so that I could tell her I'd just taken the exam. She took her technical exam to become a secretary at the age of fourteen, and after that we didn't see much of each other. We didn't have much to say. I thought about her when I went past an old public urinal. It smelled like raw chicken, with the gurgling sound of water that never stops flowing. Why aren't girls allowed to go there? For one thing, with our two feet spread apart, the bottom of our pants stops us. "I need to go . . . I need to go so bad, girl." Good old Alberte. She mimed not being able to hold it in. I never would have dared to go to that place by myself. Before going back outside, we peeked out to see if anyone was coming along the sidewalk. Men were looking at us, too, to see if we saw them coming out. It was Alberte who pointed that out to me. She had so many ideas. But when we saw each other again two years later we just said, "How're you doing?" She was already working by then, and maybe the fact that we had shown each other our pussies when we were little also created obstacles. All of that had nothing to do with the middle school exam, and while I was walking I told myself that I would remember having these thoughts after getting the results, and that they would always be connected in my mind with this stupid exam. And there was also the pharmacy where I bought my shampoo, and the face of the guy who prepared it. I wasn't thinking about boys. On the way home, which is at least a kilometer, I consulted my personal horoscope. I always have lots of them. The one in the *France-Soir* is always wrong. It's made for everybody, whereas I invent them for myself. If I walk past three white cars, it means that I passed the exam without having to take the oral. I've forgotten whether the cars told me that I would pass or not. I didn't want to go home. I drank a café au lait in the kitchen, even though I always write in my essays that it's a big bowl of hot chocolate, because that sounds better. There was nothing on TV, and besides, if I had sat down in front of the television set my mother would have said that I had been watching it too much all year so it was no surprise that I was doing it now. In my bedroom, my strange feeling came back. I had taken my mother's *Today's Women* magazine, but I couldn't get interested in it. At the foot of my bed, the red cretonne curtain with giant ladybugs on it, pulled back because of the heat, cast a colored shadow. Toward the end of the afternoon, my mother started doing her sewing in the living room. I heard her rummaging around in the sewing basket, with the needle pillow and the old dice and buttons mixed in with spools of thread. It was a soft noise. I had the feeling that I had always had it in my ears. It made me think about old age and death. The last days of middle school already seemed far away, and I couldn't see anything in front of me. A room without shadows in the summer is always strange. For the last six months I had forbidden myself to do "it," but it had been a bad day, and I didn't care if it wasn't completely dark yet. The first time I had done it, the year before, I didn't dare to look at my mother or anyone afterward. I thought they must have known about it, and it's not something normal girls are supposed to do. "A nice, straight-ahead look," my elementary school teacher used to say, "shows that you have nothing to hide." What an ordeal. It had been six months since I had done it, but it was already too late to stop. My hand smelled slightly sweet, like the tops of plants. For once, I wasn't that ashamed about it. It melted into the rest of the day, without seeming any more good or evil than the giant ladybugs. It was none of my parents' business. It even seemed like it was a good thing to do, since it brought me closer to the heart of my strangeness. The cat was scratching at the door. She stayed purring on my pillow until that evening. I liked her: she was black all over with green eyes. Did I really have the thought: "If I don't pass, I will sleep with a boy"?

When the teachers gave me my exam results, it felt like getting the middle school diploma had been a piece of cake. My father had tears in his eyes that evening after work, and even more so when, in the next day's paper, he saw my name and not the name of the daughter of Dubourg, the dentist, who had failed the written part of the test. I didn't want to tell him that a middle school diploma wasn't worth a hill of beans in terms of getting a job. I didn't want to destroy his sense of pride. My mother, shrugging her shoulders, said, "Fortunately, money doesn't buy everything. Intelligence can spring up anywhere." Personally, I've found that there are places where the grain doesn't grow so high. In my family, for example, people don't have good jobs. There's only my uncle Jean, who's a commercial artist. Or else, if they ever had any intelligence, we don't see it, which comes to the same thing. There's just a visual intelligence, and even that only sometimes. My mother kept her cool, saying, "When you work hard, you succeed. You deserved it." She played down her happiness on purpose so that I wouldn't let it go to my head and get too full of myself. She was going to repeat that sentence to me all summer: "You're getting too full of yourself." We didn't talk about my success anymore, except in front of the neighbors and the extended family. It had quite an effect on them, since they either hadn't gone on with their education or had flunked out. I don't remember how many days my feeling of pleasure lasted. I ran little errands in town, my bare shoulders showing under my dress, with my glasses in my pocket, and too bad if I ran into someone. I was riding high on my success. But I would have liked it if that success had opened up something for me right away, some new source of happiness. I didn't know what it would be, but it certainly wouldn't be this summer vacation. In other words, I wanted a reward. "You get to rest for two and a half months. Don't you realize how lucky you are? At least you'll be ready to go on the attack at the start of the new school year." "Rest." It's always rest with them, in other words doing nothing. I hate their obsession with resting. Where did it come from? On Sundays, my father doesn't know what to do with himself other than watch TV. That's what *he* means by rest. My mother had promised to buy me a dress, one that cost around a hundred francs. "We have to celebrate you passing your middle school exam. When we go to Rouen to see the eye doctor, what would you say to going shopping at Nouvelles Galeries?" The famous dress of last summer. I still look at that dress with its nearly faded grass stain, even though I know I shouldn't. It seemed like such a tiny little present. It was really cheap, and not very high quality. I don't know what else they could have afforded to buy me, or, to be honest, what exactly I was hoping for. One evening at the beginning of July a terrible storm broke out. My father was watching the Tour de France on TV and drinking his Ricard, well watered-down because he says you shouldn't drink too much when you work with machines—those who do are done for. The rain stopped. I opened the window, and the scent of the sodden neighborhood invaded my room. The air felt almost cold after the heat wave. It was the smell of things having already ended. Eight hours earlier, in the room where I took the exam, Room 5, I had seen my name on the mesh-covered bulletin board where the results were posted. I had gotten a 15 out of 20. I sat out in the sun in the school's courtyard. I wouldn't see some of my friends much anymore, or François, the bearded hall monitor. I wrote on the colored paper next to my pillow: "Anne, July 2." I was starting to get really bored, like I did every year at this time, but I couldn't tolerate it as well as I had before. It seemed unfair. School never ends: it's a real abyss. But for once, the next step was going to be a larger one. You could even say that going to high school would be like going back to square one, with other teachers and other students. My summer vacation should have marked this division in some way. I stayed in bed. It was a way of salvaging part of the day, especially with certain dreams I had been having. There was one dream about a soldier who looked like my cousin Daniel, and whose arms were wrapped around me like in a novel. I thought of something Alberte had said about how if you count thirteen stars for nine days—or maybe it was the reverse—you would dream about your future husband. Putting ice under your pillow on a Friday the thirteenth wouldn't have worked that month, since the thirteenth was a Tuesday. The stars seemed like a more serious method. I slept with my arm around my waist, thinking that might help. But I didn't dream. Every morning, my father got up to leave for work, and I went back to sleep afterward. You could hear the noise though the whole house. At six thirty I got back under the covers, plugging my ears so that I wouldn't hear the noises that traveled from room to room: his smoker's hack, his really loud spitting, the continuous settling of water in the bathrooms, the casserole banging against the stove, the spoon drawer under the table sticking and unsticking. If I unplugged my ears, I would always be able to put myself right in the middle of the noise, and I could figure out the exact moment when he left. When I heard the car start I went back to sleep. He would be working all day in this heat. At least he didn't complain. He was even kind of happy now that he was a foreman. I didn't see why I should have to feel guilty about hanging out in bed until ten o'clock. In my half-sleep, it came to me that I didn't know much about who he was outside of the house. When I was little, though, and he used to take the bus to the oil refinery, I would try to imagine how he had gone to the seaside, to Le Havre. There was always the one time a year at the seaside, with the sand squishing between your toes. On one of those Sunday excursions that were offered to the refinery workers, I had seen the metallic fences around the refinery, towers of steel ringed with black at regular intervals, with miniature stairs. The fences reminded me of the choirs of churches. I was afraid that if he fell into one of the pools of oil he had to measure the depth of, he would be in a sea of oil, and the smell of that was how his clothes smelled. I thought that all men existed just so they could have accidents, drink too much, and die. I thought that I was lucky to be a girl. Thinking back on this childish nonsense, I had the feeling that I had been more interested in him before than I was now. "Tell me about how it was on grandpa's farm," I used to ask him every evening. And one morning, when I woke up without his knowing it, I looked at his pink flesh that was completely white at the bottom of his back—which seemed so bizarre in relation to his red, swollen hands—and my curiosity was so strong that I stopped breathing. These old memories still bothered me. All I needed was ordinary and inoffensive images of him. I didn't want to have to dig deeper into all of that, into my parents and their work. He made a good living as a manual worker. We need to have them. In eighth grade we learned a poem by Verhaeren, all about the workers and everything. My father says we're all workers. I didn't ask any questions. I also never stopped to think about the fact that he had the same things as other men: male friends, stupid, slobby guys who watched girls under the old railway bridge and made those horrible drawings in the public toilets. I wasn't supposed to think about that. But even with my plugged ears, I thought about the fact that he called me "the girl" now—almost never "Anne"—and that we didn't say much to each other anymore, except in the evening when he yelled at me because I wanted to sleep with the cat. "It's not right to take cats into bed with you. It's not healthy." Every evening. I had to obey him. Finally, he left. I got up around nine o'clock. The mornings were still not too bad: brushing my hair for a quarter of an hour, getting dressed for half an hour, and then eating breakfast and listening to the radio. Everything seemed fresh for the first few hours. If I heard Whatsisname sing, at least something would have happened.

Or else the words of the next song would predict my future. But that's really tiring, and I was getting confused by all the predictions. At the end of the morning, I found myself in the kitchen with my mother. "Did you sleep well? It's going to rain again today." It had been a long time since she had said anything interesting to me. At the beginning of July, I had discovered that deep down I didn't need her, except for eating and sleeping and for buying me things. She didn't teach me anything, that was the problem. I would have liked her to tell me things or—I don't know—laugh with me, act more free, not be so pinched. Sometimes there were good teachers who talked about actual facts. We would discuss them afterward, and we wouldn't even hear the bell ring at the end of class. And with friends, we could talk for hours. With my mother, it was always the same questions. "What are you going to do this morning? Oh, good, you put your bra with the dirty clothes so that I can wash it and dry it today." When I was little, she used to do the same thing. "Why do the men who play the drums wear white gloves?" I would ask. "That's just how it's done. That's how it's always been." Never the slightest hint of an explanation. When I got my period for the first time, she didn't say much of anything, just, "You're a young woman now." But she had the little premade tampon that she had bought at the pharmacy because she thought it wasn't good to buy them at the supermarket. With the neighbors and other acquaintances, her mouth never stops running. They are conversations of no interest, ones she wouldn't even consider having with me. Maybe she's waiting for the moment when I will want to "have conversations," as she puts it. I don't think I'll ever want to. Not one of hers, I mean. I was stirring the sugar cube around in my café au lait. She was turning every which way, tinkering around, always doing stuff in the kitchen. She never thinks it's clean enough. I was smashing the sugar cube against the side of the cup because I knew that annoyed her. "Can't you stop doing that?" I saw her pick up my dress so that she could iron it on the corner of the lunch table. She was squeezed into her checkered blouse, with her wrist plunged into a bowl of water and her dry fingers spread out over the fabric. She unplugged the iron and continued to go over the dress with whatever heat was left in it, a way of economizing. "Try not to get it dirty too quickly. You don't take care of your things, my dear." Above all, there had to be order. That's all she talked about all summer. Maybe she did before too, but I had never noticed. It was like the teachers: "Don't mix everything up. Separate your arguments, young lady." I could see her again in our house on Rue Césarine, at this same table. I was coming home from elementary school, and I didn't know where to put my school satchel. It was on the day that she was salting the butter that my grandfather had given her. She was squeezing the yellow mass of butter with her hands. Brilliant strips of it squirted between her fingers, and she pressed it together, adding salt until the surface was covered with droplets of water. You knew it was completely finished when she gave three slaps to the butter with the flat of her hand. I got stains from it on my school notebooks. And the pair of shorts that we looked for everywhere on Monday, practically demolishing the chest of drawers. "Stop whining. You can put on the old pair. Who'll notice the difference?" A bunch of things that had been lost were found a month later behind the stove, all trashed. And I played handball in the kitchen. When she saw our new house, she yelled out, "Wow, look at that: brand new paint." I thought she had changed since she stopped working at the textile factory. That must be what social progress is: having a sense of order. Too bad there was no progress in her conversation. I couldn't believe the things she said. And there was no school to save me from hearing it all day long. There was only reading. I read all of my mother's *Today's Women* magazines: mostly romance stories. "Sandra Didn't Have Anyone to Love" and other titles like that made me want to read them, even though they were really silly. But once I started to get into the feelings of the story, there was nothing I could do. You don't know—yes or no?—if they're going to fall in love. I couldn't stop reading. Either they were finally going to throw themselves at each other, or they were going to die, just so it could end. Afterward, when the story ended, all of a sudden, I was abysmally sad. When the story was over, I was cast aside once again, betrayed. These days I don't read anything, because I'm not expecting anything to happen. The teacher had given us a list of very "in-te-res-ting" books. I was tremendously suspicious, since I had been taken in more than once by things that were impossibly boring. Besides, you had to go to the library and get a library card, which made me nervous. Or you could go to the bookstore, but you couldn't hang out there, because they make a fuss. At the supermarket, there are only detective books and books by Guy des Cars, which the teacher is against. I was so bored that I decided to take the plunge. I borrowed a copy of *The Stranger* from the library. I couldn't stop reading that book all day long. At some point I paused and looked around me. My bedroom seemed far away, and I couldn't understand how words could have such a strong effect on me. That evening my father got angry. It was July 8 or 9, Saint Thibault's Day: I was always checking the calendar. I had closed the blinds in my room, and when I went back into the living room, green and red stripes were streaked across my eyes. I thought about the beach, when he kills the Arab. I would have liked to write things like that, or to have lived in that way. It's easier to write about it if it really happened, and then everyone will know. My father was in a bad mood. "I'm sure you spent the whole day in front of the television, and then you watched the pop singers." He was wound up, more than I would have expected since he never drank more than one or two glasses. He started up again, "I shouldn't say anything, but you don't know what to do with yourself. You don't know how to spend your time." My mother replied that even though he wasn't there to see it, I was doing a lot of reading. Usually he kept quiet, since what I did didn't interest him. I could have sworn that he was a bit drunk. He started yelling: "Books, books. It's no way to be, with her head in books all the time. I don't think it's healthy. She's going to dry herself up. You could take a walk, or go out on your bike—I don't know." My mother came to my defense right away, talking about the things that happened to people on walks, when you went out without a purpose. It seemed like she was just being contrary, since reading isn't exactly her strong suit either. They're funny. They want me to get good grades in school, and the teachers say that reading helps with that, but I have the feeling that my parents don't really believe it. They believe in math problems and lessons. He kept pushing it: "When I was your age I was already working. I could have sat in front of a book for hours, too." She got mad, saying he was being thickheaded. "Do you think it's a good thing to have to start working at fourteen? Do you really want to see your daughter working in a factory? Let her rest and read. She's not hurting anyone." I always feel awkward when they fight about me. It's as if they weren't talking about me, but about some other Anne, the good little mommy-and-daddy's girl. Basically, it's like they're making a fuss about nothing. Besides, on that evening I felt that I was a phony. There was no point in pretending I was innocent. I knew that reading all day was soft, and even a bit dirty: especially that kind of book, which stays with you afterward, unlike romance novels. Maybe they were right to think that reading is dangerous—more than TV. The proof is that on that day, after I read my book, my parents seemed ridiculous to me, and if I hadn't held myself back I could easily have told them everything I felt. But you shouldn't talk that way to your parents. It would be too awful. They're so nice, and they don't have a lot of money. You have to be understanding. I don't know where I had heard that phrase, but when you think about it, you're doubly trapped in this situation. You have to keep your mouth shut all the time so that you won't hurt their feelings. For example, there was the thing with the lace dress. It wasn't the one I wanted the most, and yet I had to thank my mother three times as much as you would have to thank parents who could've bought several of them without batting an eye. It was completely unfair. Even so, I dared to add, "What do you want me to do, other than read and watch TV?" "You could find a friend to go to the pool with you." "All the other girls are away on vacation." I was lying— Gabrielle Bouvet hadn't gone away—but I didn't want to go into details. It's the general idea that matters, and my mother always says to look above yourself and not below yourself if you want to make your way in life. Gabrielle is definitely below, and my mother doesn't like her that much because she thinks she's strange. "Friendships are fine and dandy, but they're not worth the risks that come with certain relationships," they always say. They didn't answer me. My father dug himself deeper into his armchair with his glass of not-very-watered-down Ricard, and my mother wiped the top of the stove with rapid little strokes, pouting into a mixing bowl. Later, she concluded, "You want to have everything, but wait until you see what the real world is like." It was that sentence that annoyed me the most. I was about to turn sixteen, and they didn't even realize it. At dinner I kept my mouth shut. When I got back to my bedroom, I had already finished *The Stranger*, and I didn't know what to do next. I glued my eyes to the window blinds, to the gravel in the alley, and to the ends of privet hedges. I felt peculiar and sad. The argument with my parents seemed unimportant. It was as if reading the book had divided me in two. I sat on the bed in my bathrobe, and I looked into my dressing-table mirror. I started making faces at myself. I squinted. I was a real nutcase. "Be careful or you'll stay like that." What a joke. Maybe I was a bit crazy after all. You never know. I felt like I was the only person in the house. In middle school we kids didn't always like each other, but at least we were together. That was reassuring: it gave us reference points. With your parents, you don't have any reference points. I was suddenly afraid of being abnormal, and I got undressed with slow, deliberate gestures, like in a movie. But the more I thought about it, the more I felt like I was just showing off. If they only knew. "I've always said that all that studying and reading books goes to her head. What's the point of her going to high school if she sacrifices her health doing it?" "Be quiet! Do you want her to be like us, starting work at fourteen? She's the only one in the family who's gotten this far." I cried. I didn't want to stop, because crying made me feel less crazy. If only I could have talked to them about the book I had just read. But they wouldn't have thought that was normal either. When the three of us watch something on TV, they always say "that was good," or "that was stupid," or "that didn't make sense," and then, "Let's go to bed: it's a school day tomorrow." Then he turns off the television. That was certainly how things went for the next few days. I became just like everyone else again. They were right that *The Stranger* was only literature, but I was still sad to see the bizarre thoughts I'd been having drift away. I was sad about becoming normal again. In other words, I was so bored that I watched TV for three afternoons and evenings in a row. I even watched the ads. I remembered how when I was little there was no TV at our house, and during the vacations I would leaf through *Today's Women* and tell myself stories about the ads. I built myself a house filled with all the products that were mentioned, and I had a dress from La Redoute and slippers made by André. I would start all over again with each issue. I even swallowed the anticonstipation pills. The only thing I left out were the dentures. But doing that wasn't much fun. I was ashamed of liking to look at ads. Luckily, my mother started waitressing three mornings a week at the Café de la Petite Vitesse. As soon as she would attach her bag to the handlebars of her bike and push down on the pedal, leaning forward—I could see everything through the window, and the times when it took her a long time to leave I shuddered at the thought of how annoying she was—then, off she went, and I felt a terrific sense of freedom. The house was mine. My father and mother were gone. It was a dream come true! I wandered around the rooms of the house, went out into the yard, and—too bad I fell back into my old habits so fast—ended up opening all the cupboards and the fridge. I stuffed myself with cookies and the ends of cold cuts, cutting them in a beveled shape so that they wouldn't notice. I thought, "You're going to turn into a barrel." I would have eaten all the fish in the sea just to make the time pass. I imagined the worst I could do if they weren't coming back, but since they were only gone for half a day, there was nothing I could do that would be really exciting. I couldn't even rearrange a piece of furniture, except in my bedroom. You're always a tenant in your parents' house. I looked around everywhere, but there were no secrets: no letters, no hidden objects. The only things I uncovered were some pay stubs and the checkbook from the credit union. Not very interesting, even though they never talked about those things in front of me. One day, I had asked myself if our house was beautiful or not. I decided that it was good enough. In any case, I couldn't imagine another. It would have meant having other parents. I listened to the same record three or four times, because it was the only time I could do that without attracting comments. "What are you getting out of this song? You're going to make yourself stupid, my dear, you're really going to make yourself stupid. I'll never understand the pleasure you get from hearing the same song ten times." Listening to a record for the second time, and then listening to it again after that, you can narrow it down more and more. You can get to the point where you grasp something in it, some perfection. You don't find it the first time. It's often the second time, and then it falls away again. I didn't want to listen to that song anymore that day. And in the afternoon, I could hear all the cars on the national highway that must have been going toward the beaches at Veules-les-Roses, which really ruined everything for me when I thought about it. Long before the day when I ran into Gabrielle Bouvet, I had been thinking about her, about what she must be doing. I imagined that she had friends in her apartment building. I, on the other hand, was all alone. If I ran into her in town, I would stop and talk to her. There's always more going on when there are two of you. It would be more of a sure thing than my horoscopes, which were always wrong—no better than counting stars or putting ice under the pillow. I tried on my dress, put on makeup, and did my chest lifts. I sat back down again, discouraged at being the only person who could see me. Everything happened outdoors, not inside the house, and my mother was obsessed with keeping me inside. I would gladly have gone to the pool, even by myself: at least I would find other girls there. "But you told me they had all left! You might just as well do your tanning in the yard, in your swimsuit. Where no one can see you." She had forgotten about the neighbor, thinking that kids don't remember anything. He came to stalk me, the old pervert (who wasn't really so old), with his way of hopping over the shallot bed with one big step, then quietly stopping behind the rows of green beans, crouched down as if he was weeding a spot. I didn't have my glasses on. He could get an eyeful, as my father atrociously puts it, whereas I couldn't see a thing. At the pool, the voyeurs seemed a bit less menacing, more authorized in a way. There, in the yard, I was disgusted by the little noises he would make with his mouth, and his secret trampling just on the other side of the wire mesh. I tried not to imagine it and to act like it never happened, but it was hard. Once a guy has taken out his dick, you think he is going to do it every time. It becomes a habit. It made me laugh to think that my parents really didn't know the number of perverts there were, including some who were parents themselves. When I saw their kids, I always asked myself, "Did he do . . . to them?" I met so many of them when I was in the projects with Alberte. They started to come out in March like the primroses, prowlers who had strange eyes with a little, fixed gleam in them. Other than that, they were very ordinary, though they were a bit more shy than other people. Their problem was their outfits: you could easily see what they were up to. Alberte would say, "Look, he . . ." They were always buttoning, unbuttoning, and feeling around in their pockets, standing behind untrimmed hedgerows pretending to be cutting them, or mowing a grassy bank, or taking a mean-looking dog on a walk. They did everything slowly: their steps, their gestures. What was that one guy getting ready to do? He smelled like earth and burnt wood. I ran until the sound of my shoes pounded in my head, with him far away and looking like a scarecrow. I was so happy to have escaped that time, having seen almost nothing while nearly seeing everything. I thought about Alberte, who was never afraid. Or maybe it was that when there were two of us we felt strong, or they were more wary of us. They would just say, "Hey, girls, how ya doin'?" We said hello to the dog—"good doggy, good boy"—patting it, and he laughed at the other end of the leash, looking at us with his awful eyes. "Careful, he's going to piss on your leg if you tickle him." I would have liked to be at the pool on cement, tanning and swimming in real sunlight. My mother must not have known that the lech was in the yard. What was even worse was that I was getting tan with only my parents to see it.

A little before the July 14 holiday, I was woken up by a gurgling sound in the bathroom. I recognized my father from the sound of violent spitting up. I immediately pulled the covers up over my head. That sound always upsets me: I get scared when they're sick. Their faces change, like they're crazy. "God, please let my parents live until I get married and have two children. Then it won't be as sad." I stayed under my sheet, smothered by it. I was thinking about a picture in my history book. A guy had fallen at the foot of his bed, with his legs spread apart. I didn't dare to go check on my father. My mother's the one who deals with sickness. That's fine with me: it's too disgusting. The day had started out badly. I had enough trouble to deal with, and now this would change my sunbathing routine. My mother said that he had indigestion, that his stomach was upset from eating charcuterie. They had to call Dr. Louvel, "Old Man Berdouillette," so that my father could take a day off work. That's what we call our doctor, which always amuses my parents. My father got out of bed to eat dinner, even though he was feeling sick and didn't eat much. That annoyed me because all he talked about was his lack of appetite, not about any kind of real sickness where you can imagine something terrible happening. It wasn't worth all this trouble just for a misplaced fart. Louvel, the old monkey on wheels, came over to the house that evening. He didn't scare me like he used to. Now he just annoyed me. He drove a *deux chevaux*, so apparently he wasn't too proud of how much money he made. What disgusted me was what went on between him, my mother, and me. He put his hand like a visor over his eyes, acting shocked to see me so grown up. He spoke to my parents with an air of superior mockery that they never seemed to notice. And I never knew what to say to him, since it didn't matter what I said. My mother told him, "You know, she passed her middle school diploma exam, and she'll be going to high school next year." "Well that's good, very good. You're making something out of your daughter. She'll be someone." My mother went on talking in a whisper. She whispers when she's around certain people, important people. With us, it's just the opposite: she'd rather yell. "Don't you agree that it's important nowadays to have an education?" "How right you are, my good lady." I was sure that Berdouillette took us for yokels. He had examined me when I felt tired after the exam, and had given me dietary supplements. She had watched as he tapped me on the back, glued his head to me underneath my lifted top, and pressed on each side of my stomach. I got goosebumps in spite of the heat. What did she think was happening when he put his fingers down below? I could only see the crown of his head. His mouth was tightly closed, trying to look serious. Otherwise, it would have been obvious that he was a pig. He hissed, "Everything all right? Does the plumbing work every month?" I didn't know if he expected her or me to reply. She answered right away: "Yes, everything is fine . . . fine." She started talking about how many sanitary pads I used. She really should have let me talk about that. "Everything has been regular from the start. Completely normal, doctor." "That's what we like to see." I hate doctors. Maybe you should go to a different one each time. He gave me calcium pills, and he gave my father some powder for his stomach. While we were eating, my father asked what was wrong with me. "Just fatigue," my mother answered. That was all she said. The subject of my health is only between her and me now. My father burst out roughly, and perhaps with some Ricard on his breath: "I DIDN'T KNOW ABOUT THAT! No one told me anything about her becoming a woman. That makes me really sad!" I felt ashamed. I wanted to leave. In two years, she had never told him about it! How had she managed to hide my dirty laundry from him in a basket in the bathroom? She hasn't been able to see much of anything herself for three years. I know she does it, since I rummage through everything. She blushed. He seemed bothered. It was so embarrassing to see them behaving strangely because of me. To think that he had just learned about it, that it was all new to him, and that the news might be hard for him. He looked ugly and gray from his indigestion. I decided to do the same thing to her as she had been doing to him: I would hide the little colored packets and then take them to the outside garbage bin myself. "You should never wash your hair when you're indisposed." I would carry that sickly word, "indisposed," which made you think about pains and nausea, like a talisman. I would never confide anything to her again. I would rather have been at summer camp, or anywhere else. I brought the cat into my bed, but after a minute she decided to go out the window. She ran out. "There's no way to keep her inside," my father had said.

I HAVE THE SENSE THAT IT WAS ONLY BY LUCK THAT I MET Gabrielle Bouvet in town, and that we became closer friends than we had been in middle school. I wasn't wearing my glasses, but we were on the same sidewalk. I prefer to think of it as good luck, because if I thought that it was just because there were no other girls from middle school in the neighborhood, it would mean that we met simply through a process of elimination. That would change my perspective too much, and it would be a sad comment on our friendship, even though it might be true. She had the legs of a cyclist and was even darker than Alberte. I was never able to be friends with girls I thought were pretty. Actually, I wonder what it was that connected us. Outside of school, it's not easy to start conversations. You end up talking about personal things right away, which makes it awkward. We hung out together in front of the stores for a while. I thought I was better than her—which was a very agreeable thought—but it seems that intelligence and grades in school are of secondary importance in these situations. As if to prove it, we were accosted by some guys on motor scooters who knew Gabrielle, neighbors of hers. I didn't think they were so great-looking, even though they were at least eighteen. Gabrielle forgot to introduce us, but one of the guys put his very sweaty hand on my shoulder. Another one said, "Hey, man, don't be a jerk," and started mugging on his bike. I wasn't sure I wanted this particular reward for getting my diploma. They asked us if we wanted to go to the July 14 fair in Saint-Pierre. A lot of the girls from middle school never went to it. For them, it's just a low-class fair. But you have to make do with the opportunities that present themselves. I could see it all: the bumper cars, standing cheek to cheek at the shooting gallery, walking back and forth on whatever street was the most hidden and deserted, or going to the old railway bridge. But which of the three guys would it be? I was getting really excited. On July 14 it rained like cows pissing, and for the first time in the whole vacation I was actually going to be going out. I waited for Gabrielle to come and pick me up. I watched by the window. It was a bit humiliating to have to wait for her, so I started to read. I thought that the sentence I was reading when she appeared on her bike would predict what would happen that afternoon. I was always looking for signs. I had already been waiting for that bitch for over an hour when my mother said, "Your beautiful friend is making you wait." I was listening to music that was coming from far away, the air smelled like rain, and it seemed to me that I would always be sitting like that, waiting for something that had fallen through. I was thinking about *The Stranger* again, even though I hadn't killed anyone. Finally, she arrived. I didn't dare get mad at her for being late. She wasn't what mattered: it was only the fair. It was important not to ruin things. At first, I was afraid to move into the crowd. I don't know what Gabrielle thought: you don't tell each other those kinds of things. But the boys had come, a sign that a kind of complicity was growing between us. There wasn't much else between us, and if you don't count boys and sexual things we weren't really friends. It wasn't like with Alberte. Although that didn't really prevent Alberte and me from becoming estranged from each other. Maybe she was angry with me because of everything she dared to tell me and show me. At the Saint-Pierre fair, I didn't feel like I was there with Gabrielle. The boys left, saying they wanted to go to a dance instead. I was disappointed. We slipped into the noise of the fair, and I decided that—screw it—I wasn't going to just stand there like a statue, as my mother says on these occasions. Gabrielle and I went straight to the bumper cars, where all the boys are, without saying that was why. I would have gladly stayed there the whole time. Some guys were chasing us in their cars and bumping into the side of our car. We saw them coming toward us with horrible triumphant smiles as we heard the click-click sound of the metal shafts and they slammed full tilt into us, making us all fall halfway out of our cars. My favorite moment was when they were going to hit us and I knew that we couldn't avoid them because they were going so fast, and I screamed in anticipation. Afterward, they shot us lascivious looks. That's a word we liked to use that day, a word from books. We called all the men "lascivious," and that brought Gabrielle and me closer. Sometimes we couldn't detach ourselves from their cars, which was unpleasant since it was wasted time. They thought that we got tangled up with them on purpose, that we were running after them, trying to get into their pants. I didn't look at them anymore: they were actually really ugly. It was only the shock of getting hit that I liked, and then driving through the spaces between the cars, with all the guys standing around the sides of the track, and going by them at the level of their knees. Every time the cars would stop moving, the screech of their brakes would pound our eardrums. It had been a real dream, and when it ended our pleasure came to a halt as well. It took two or three spins around the fairground to find that pleasure again. When we had been there for an hour, I didn't have much cash left, and neither did Gabrielle. Actually, she had even less than me. But it's hard to talk about money. We get it from our parents, so it's connected with them, and we would never dare to ask each other how much our parents make. We still hadn't found any interesting boys. We went from stand to stand. For a laugh, we did the horoscope: it cost two francs. You had to pull the handle, a piece of pink paper fell out, and then you had to wet a silver circle with your saliva to see your future Johnny Boy appear. Gabrielle's had the face of a habitual offender, and mine was at least thirty years old. We laughed hard, although it was a bit forced. It leaves a bad taste in your mouth when gross things like that happen, even if you don't believe in them. And then there was the Superstar Raffle. We didn't buy tickets, but there was the guy dressed in black who does impersonations of different singers. I'd been coming to the Saint-Pierre fair for five years, and I remember thinking—that one year when my parents tried to win a bottle of sparkling wine or a doll—that he was cute. He didn't impersonate the same stars anymore. He always had red painted around his mouth, almost up to his nose, and he walked a bit hunched over. Between songs, he sold raffle tickets. I thought he recognized me from two years ago when I couldn't stop looking at him while he was doing Charles Aznavour. Alberte once said a terrible thing: "When you love a man you should be willing to eat his shit." I felt ashamed at being able to change my opinion about someone so much in just two years. But there was nothing I could do about it now. I would never be able to choose anyone. Now, I wouldn't even have held that poor loser's hand. The afternoon went on. There were just ordinary people at the fair. We only saw one teacher: he looked like he was just there to watch other people having fun. It would've been better if he hadn't come at all. We had to keep a big crowd of people between him and us. We cut between the trailers, in front of the water coolers. It was funny: we felt the fair more strongly after we had left it for five minutes. We ate some donut balls, and some guys followed us, asking if the "balls" were good. They were bent over with laughter. "I have two more of them. Should we trade?" Gabrielle shot me a glance out of the corner of her eye to see if I understood. I felt that I could laugh then, because we had understood the same thing. We started laughing again every time we raised the donuts to our mouths. But after hearing their dirty talk, I didn't want those guys to stay with us, and I didn't want what would come after. Girls always talk about the little, hidden things they use to attract boys, and boys are always ready to talk about their balls. Also, they were treating us like pieces of meat. We were already far away from them, and I was thinking about my face, my legs, and the way of moving that is me, Anne. It didn't make any sense to me. By five o'clock we had gone around the fair at least ten times and spent our last coins on the bumper cars so that we wouldn't feel like we'd missed anything. I don't know how we calculated it, but we decided that all the guys we had seen were ugly. And then everyone started to look ugly to me. The guys with red lips were braying at the Superstar concert, and the women who "had to make their living," as my parents put it, were dancing in their swimsuits. It always smells like piss at fairs, and the songs are a year behind, which makes you feel lost in time. I was getting more and more melancholic, but I still loved it. It was fun to lift your head up toward the sky when you were all pressed up against each other. I thought about God, not the God of the mass and the Virgin wearing a washed-out blue dress, but the one who was dripping with sadness, the one who maybe never existed. The one who left us alone. It felt like I didn't have parents either. Suddenly, I felt old. These kinds of thoughts make you feel older, because you've never had them before. It seemed to me that I could understand why people write books, better than I had when we read them in school. They write them because there are fairs full of noise, and because they suddenly come apart. We had to go home. It's terrible to have to leave the crowd behind, with the music still playing, especially when you have to go back across narrow streets that are blocked by trailers. And no boyfriend today, my sweet Gabrielle. But I wasn't going to cry about it. I was getting along better and better with Gabrielle, and being able to go out was what mattered most. My mother made a huge fuss about the fact that we were half an hour late: "No decent girls are out at this hour." She inspected me, and luckily I had put my glasses back on. I wish she would at least say clearly what she's afraid of. She never does. Just saying it would burn her throat. My father wasn't home, so she kept going: "We let you go out, and this is how you repay us." You would have to be parents to figure that the way to repay them was to come back on time. It's either because they're bored or because they're worried about you. She was still wearing her Sunday clothes, with her top that never stayed tucked into her skirt, and her zipper that was always coming down. That pink spot in the middle of her back, with the flesh exposed for everyone to see, was always an ordeal for me. "But no, silly girl, that's my best outfit," she would say. And then there was that awful gesture of pulling out her skirt when it got stuck between her butt cheeks. And that afternoon, in some cemetery, she had crouched down behind a monument to the dead, looked to see if anyone was coming, and then pissed, saying "Wow, that was a flood!" If I was going to accept her ideas, she would have to be perfect. My mother, with her dirty memories. I peeled potatoes with her to soften her up so that she would let me see Gabrielle again. In the Tour de France, a different guy was wearing the yellow jersey. She started to calm down. Yes, she was afraid of me going out, but only in a vague sort of way. She must not have known that if a girl goes to a fair it means she's trying to get picked up. It had been a good day. At dinner, they talked about the cousins they had gone over to see that afternoon. They spent the whole evening making comparisons. If they decorated their house in that way, it meant they must have had to cut back on food, with what they earn. I said that was a bad calculation to make. My father agreed. "And educating the girl is going to cost money. Instead of spending money like that, he should spend it on his kids." They expanded on the topic through the whole meal. For them, there was no summer vacation and no Saint-Pierre fair. They always kept their eyes on jobs, on education, on studying, on the future—as if the present didn't count for anything. In a way, it would have been better for my father if he could have jumped right into the future, or else locked me up to make sure that I would make it there in good condition. It occurred to me that maybe it was their dream to lock me up, since they made such a fuss about a tiny bit of lateness. There had been the start of middle school, then the next school year, and then there would be the start of high school, and then another school year. And then what? You couldn't go on like that for your whole life. It was strange for me to see myself with them that evening, with my mother blah-blah-blahing about the cousins. They should never go to anyone else's house. They always come back unhappy when it seems nicer than theirs. When I looked on the calendar, I saw that only one-fifth of the summer vacation was over. That night I cried.

THE TRAIN SMELLED LIKE COFFEE, AND THE SEATS SMELLED like fake leather. I like the smell of trains in the summer, but this was just a half-hour train ride with my mother to see the eye doctor. Sitting across from her, I wondered if we could get through the day without her starting to grumble. The smallest little thing and she would immediately get into a bad mood that would last until evening. I didn't know if I was happy about this outing, with a day stretching out in front of me that was too full of errands and of walking next to her. She was always ready to complain that I walked too slowly. Also, I was wearing one of last year's dresses, which wasn't low cut and was a bit little-girlish, but which I was forced to wear so that she wouldn't ask questions. That ruined everything for me. We went onto a quiet street that was paved with fat cobblestones. There was a sign saying, "Dr. Cochet: Optometrist." We rang the bell. I don't like it when you have to wait. Maybe they do it to you on purpose. There was a maid dressed in black and white. "Do you have an appointment with the doctor?" She was suspicious, and she had an almost superior air. I wondered what it was based on. She led us up a staircase that was so deeply waxed on the sides that I was afraid to step off the carpet. My mother tried to walk in a composed way and not slip. She would have hurt herself. That was what they wanted: to see if you would make it to the top without falling down. And the maid was in on it, with a smile like the one the nurse has when she gives you your shots. The carpet ended at the waiting room, where you had to hurl yourself onto a parquet floor, which creaked. It was disturbing. There were lots of people waiting in armchairs. Like them, we had to wait for an hour and a half without complaining, just sighing, "Ooh la la." I had looked through all the magazines that were spread out on a gilded table with twisted legs. They could have furnished three rooms with just the collection of stuff that was in this one waiting room: sculpted chests, two display cabinets full of Japanese statues, and at least three meters of lace curtains. The silence made me uncomfortable. People were watching each other. Everything seemed very far away. We were the spectators of a harmonious world that was stuffed with objects. But we were only spectators. Just to be clever, I whispered to my mother, "Is the inside of our cousins' house this beautiful?" "You're crazy! You can't compare it with a specialist like this. He can afford to buy beautiful things, no matter what they cost. Hundreds of thousands, so be quiet!" She was just guessing: she wasn't really interested in the actual price of things. She would rather just admire them. In this case, the difference between this waiting room and our house didn't bother her. On the contrary, it might have proved to her that he was an important specialist. On the other hand, in the case of our cousins from Le Havre who wanted to display their wealth for everyone to see, she couldn't stand it. Basically, the greater the difference, the more she could accept it. Why had she chosen to come to this doctor? He was famous, and he had saved the sight of some bigwig or other. A miracle! Better than Lourdes! Except that in my case I was only a bit nearsighted, so it wasn't worth this much trouble. "What's your name? Sit down over there." He put some atrocious black binoculars on my nose, and then he put tons of different pieces of glass into them really quickly, saying, "Better or worse? Answer!" I wasn't keeping up, and he got mad. "You must know what you're seeing!" My mother said, "Answer the doctor." It was horrible: she was treating me like I was a little girl. He wrote out a prescription. "You hear what the doctor says: you mustn't take off your glasses." But she was saying it for his benefit. She quickly riffled through her handbag. It was never fast enough when it was a question of paying and she didn't think she had enough money. By the time we left, I was feeling unhappy. I could have killed that old fart who addressed me as *tu* and who treated us like a pair of old socks. And we didn't open our mouths to talk back to him. I'm not used to talking back to teachers or people who are above me, and that's also probably how my parents feel when they just accept everything that happens to them. But she could've at least come to my defense and said that he should take the time for me to try on all the glasses. We were paying for them, after all. Instead, she wanted to please him, to make nicey-nicey, even though that wouldn't do anything for her once she got to the bottom of the staircase. She thought it was all right for him to take on his grand airs with us, for him to yell at me, even though she always said that you couldn't let yourself get pushed around, that you had to defend yourself. But against who? This was exactly the kind of overblown show-off that I would have liked to squash. But not her. I could see that she liked to get in good with important people, and it seemed to me that my parents were wrong to do that, since it would never get them anywhere. It was the same way with teachers and school counselors. She always took their side. "You know, you have to take her in hand if she doesn't listen to you. You have to punish her." There was the thrashing I got in eighth grade when the teacher told her I hadn't turned in a homework assignment. The teacher was cool about it, but not her. She took it upon herself to hit me. And when I was in elementary school she used to say, "I'm going to tell your teacher. She'll punish you." I believed it. I believed this threat she made over a theft from the sugar bowl. Would she really go and tell the teachers at school about it? I was always scared that she would. The day was growing gray. My mother sensed that something was wrong. "Don't worry. That doctor is a bit rough, but he's right: you have to wear your glasses. Otherwise, what's the point in coming at all? Do you think this is fun for me?" She kept it up all the way to the door of the Nouvelles Galeries. The worst part is that I can never get my parents to stop once they get started on their song and dance. I wanted to buy another lace dress, one that was low cut both in front and in back. But in the aisles full of dresses, I knocked hangers off and fiddled around without being able to choose. And my mother was standing next to me, saying, "Make a good choice! We're not coming back here. Aren't there enough dresses for you to find something?" Her good intentions were gradually falling by the wayside. On top of everything else, I was being too indecisive. Looking at myself in the changing-room mirror, I wondered what would make me look the most desirable, as they say in romance novels. But that wasn't it, exactly. I was trying to look like someone, like Céline maybe, and I made sure that the fabric hugged my waist and my breasts really well. It was impossible for my mother to suspect what I was thinking about as I turned around and around in front of the saleslady—"That's a really fresh, pretty dress"—or maybe she was showing me that she didn't really want to see the truth, which was that with a little effort you could guess everything that was under the fabric. I bought the red one, but by the time we got outside, I wished it had been the white one. Buying, always buying. My parents were right to begrudge me things. I wasn't as happy with it as I had hoped. There's a strange dead time right after you come out of the Nouvelles Galeries with your little package. You never feel like you got enough for your money. I would have had to buy ten dresses at a time. Then it would seem less important which ones I got, and I would feel lighter. Whereas now, my purchase had already become a drama by the time we left the store. "I hope you'll at least wear it, and it won't stay in your closet," she said, for some reason or other. "And try to pay attention to what I'm saying." And it wouldn't end there. A simple purchase haunts us for days and weeks on end. You start to ask yourself if you made a mistake, to the point where the dress starts to seem soiled or out of fashion. These things aren't important, but they were the only things I had to think about. I only had two dresses, so it was bound to be important. It was demoralizing. And then there was the pudgy eye doctor who had stuck a half dozen frames on my ears while he pushed back my hair. And when my mother took out her wallet, I didn't want to think about it too much. I would have felt too guilty. They're the ones who earn the money, not me. The poor woman. I had already decided to hide those beautiful glasses that cost twenty thousand francs at the bottom of my bag. Seeing her wallet didn't change that. And then there were the records she had promised to get me. She mispronounced the name of my favorite singer three times, giving me yet another reason for not being able to stand her. All afternoon there was this game of cat and mouse between the two of us just so that she could make me sweat. No, she wasn't any worse than other mothers. She said, menacingly, "You don't seem happy. You always want such extravagant things!" And then, acting all sweet again, "Should we buy ourselves a pastry?" She even acted like she was my friend, saying, "I don't know if you're like me or not, but . . ." Rouen tires me out, trotting from one store to another. I gave her the cold shoulder. In any case, the day had been ruined, since any kind of pleasure always turns sour with the two of them. I don't know whose fault it is. That evening, on the train, I stood in the corridor while she found a seat next to the window. She had the full shopping nets on her knees, and the powder on her face was patchy. I felt sorry for her. I'd been so mean. She was right. She had read a story once—I think it was in her *Intimité* magazine—about an awful girl who tore up her clothes on purpose just to make her parents suffer. She told the story in front of my father at the dinner table. "Try never to be like that, you understand?" My eyes stung in horror. I stole the magazine, but I didn't understand anything except that the girl in question was me, Anne. I hid the magazine in a rusted pipe in the yard, and every time I played next to it, I felt that it was a proof of my meanness, rolled up like a parchment until the day of my death. Or my parents' death. In the train corridor, men passed behind me, and I flattened myself against the window. It was only old guys. They were treating me more and more like a nasty girl. When I think about it, I can't say that wasn't true. I should have thanked her more for the presents: for the dress and the records she had bought. I don't know why, but I just couldn't do it. Before, when we lived on Rue Césarine, she would say, "Tell me how much you love your mommy?" "This much, this much, this much . . . as much as the sky!" "And what about your daddy?" "This little, this little . . . as little as the tip of my fingernail!" She would swell with happiness, and he would laugh. It seemed all right to him. When she used to work at the textile factory, she was so wiped out on Sunday afternoons that she would sleep until five o'clock, fully dressed except for her stockings. I slept next to her. We were like two dogs packed into the same crate. Her body was wide and perfect, and there were pink garters, with the metal buckles unfastened, which danced around in a funny way on her skin whenever she moved. I pretended to sleep. When she woke up, around five o'clock, she didn't talk for a long time. She looked for her slippers, and then she went onto her throne in the bathroom, with the door open and a smell of bleach. I watched her. There was a shadow, and then all at once the skirt was pulled down, and there was no way of knowing the shape of what I had glimpsed. Her body didn't make me sick to my stomach then. When I dressed up in her big dress with mauve flowers on it, there was the smell of the kitchen and of her sweat. When I watched her cleaning herself up, the straps of her dress slid down to the middle of her arms, and her beautiful legs were smooth and hairless. I found all men ugly, without even makeup on their faces to make them look better. How could she love him, with his rough and ruddy skin? These images seemed far away now. She was half asleep leaning on the Nouvelles Galeries packages. It was too late. I didn't like sleeping in the space behind her back in the afternoon anymore, and there was "that thing," which she called her "crougnougnous" as if it was a dirty animal. I never saw it. I would have covered my eyes rather than see it. Remembering what it had been like didn't explain anything. There was something that I couldn't stand any longer in these images of her and me. Or maybe it was my whole childhood that I couldn't stand. I agree with them: it's exams and school that make you move forward in life. For example, my new dress was the future, and what happened later would have been different if I hadn't gotten it. But it doesn't matter how much my parents talk about how they want the future to be: they'll always represent my childhood and the past. It seems that being on the train leads to reflections.

IT WAS JULY 18. THAT EVENING I CRIED, SEEING HOW TIME was passing and how I was young for no reason. That afternoon, I had watched the neighbor woman from across the way hanging up the wash. There were meters of laundry, what with all the kids they have. I've never liked big families, that jumble of eyes and stomachs, and doorknobs that stick to your fingers. She came out to check if the laundry was dry, quickly rustling each item. Sometimes she took something down. An hour later, she came back and gathered up the rest with a snap of her wrist, along with the clothespins. This neighbor woman didn't seem any better off than I was, except that she didn't have to think about it like I did, so she wasn't bored. I can tell that adults are never bored. Is there a moment when you suddenly start feeling like your life is filled up, like there's no room for thinking anymore? "You don't know what to do with yourself, my poor girl. Just wait till you start working!" My father slept in on Sundays because he was so wiped out from work. "You'll have plenty of time to figure out what it's like. Take advantage of your freedom." I still couldn't figure out if they liked working. I was confused by what they said. He bragged about putting in overtime at the factory. They yelled at me one day because I said that I wouldn't have a profession, that I would just travel all the time and stay at hotels. If I had said that again I would have needed bandages for my head. Maybe they work for my sake. I'm not going to have any children. I tried to invent things to do that looked like a job. I woke up at nine and made the bed, ate breakfast at ten, dusted at ten fifteen, and studied English at one. It all seemed fake. There was no need to take those activities seriously. Even studying seemed pointless, since I wasn't going back to school for another two months. It must be the money you make that lets you know you it's a job. Or it could be the fact that you're doing something useful. What I was doing seemed like a kid's game. I was either playing at being the student I would be in two months or playing the housewife cleaning her house. At least my mother gets paid for cleaning up at the Petite Vitesse, whereas I don't get a cent for cleaning my room. Even so, I went through my drawers and made decisions about what to throw away. By the end of July, I wouldn't open them anymore: I would know all my clothes by heart. I gave up on inventing jobs and on trying on my dresses to see if they would look good to anyone. One dusty evening it started to rain, with big raindrops. When the rain starts, the birds always get excited and start chirping. The neighbor woman had taken down her laundry. I wasn't bored. I wanted to tell myself stories. I'm not really sure if I that's what I wanted. I don't know if I wanted to tell stories about the guys I'd seen the other day on motor scooters, and, further back, about certain guys from middle school I'd thought about. All of them melted together into a soft background that took my breath away. But not a single *real* boy on the horizon, nothing to do for the whole endless stretch of summer vacation, and Gabrielle wasn't coming over. "I don't have a cent, my dear." Alberte and I used to laugh as if we would never stop, in those days. I didn't want to write about shameful things. I was done with those dirty scribblings on the inside page of a protective notebook, those words that you can't find in the dictionary and that I couldn't stop myself from writing in very small letters, but that filled me with fear at the same time. No, this was different. I felt that there was something I needed to write. It was something that was contained in this room and that was connected with what was in it, with my stupid life, and with the birds that were celebrating the rain. And with all these desires I had. How would I go about describing the town, the neighborhood, and then myself? After all, we're not characters in a novel, that's pretty clear, and nothing ever happens to me. Later, when I had lived for a long time or when I'd slept with a boy, I thought I would be able to express myself. I could see that I lacked both the language and the things I needed to know about. But I was wrong. My mother had such a hard time when she had to write a letter, a greeting card, or a note to a teacher. She turned her pen in little circles in the air above the paper and then suddenly threw herself into the task, sitting up very straight, with her eyes lowered. She says that she has a hard time putting words together, that it either works or it doesn't—you just have to know the trick of it. But there are certainly models in books: for example, I discovered that *The Stranger* sometimes talked about ordinary little things. But you would have had to change them into things in your own life, and then it would get boring right away. Finding it impossible to write, I drank a café au lait at four o'clock while my mother was writing out her shopping list. My writing wasn't going anywhere. And besides, I wanted to be able to go straight to important things, and the events in my life and my feelings about them barely filled a page. You can't just write about how pissed off you are, and even if you do it's too limited a subject. I tried to write, in spite of it all. I wrote in the third person: it seemed safer, in case I had delicate things to say. When I had written three pages, I didn't want to go on. It was like the beginning of a story in *Intimité*, where two people meet on a train, in the first-class compartment, but the girl went into the wrong train car by mistake. You had to write it that way so that she could have a CEO fall in love with her. In fact, I didn't have any delicate details to talk about. I was getting bored, and I let myself get distracted by something, and I lost my train of thought, and then I lost track of the subject and even the words themselves. I had gotten very far away from the rain and the squareness of backyards, and from the stories that were hidden somewhere in these walls. I scrunched the paper up, and then I thought it would be better to cut it up into little pieces. If my mother found my rough draft, she would pester me about it. "Is what you wrote here true or made up?" The made-up parts would matter to her much more than the true parts. My parents were always suspicious. "What are you doing, sweetheart? Tell me." "I'm not doing anything." "Are you writing lies?" "No, it's just for fun." "It's not for school, then?" In their opinion, writing was dangerous, like touching your privates or grimacing like a dingo. "Stop doing that. You'll just make yourself unhappy!" They would have asked me what the point was. "These kinds of stories don't serve any purpose." At that moment, my attempt at writing literature ended. First of all, it wasn't literature: that wasn't the word for it. I wanted something to happen, that was all, and nothing was happening. I started worrying about dinner. Lunch didn't matter, since my mother and I always ate on the fly. Fortunately, I'm always hungry. I looked at the tomatoes and eggs for the first few minutes of dinner without thinking about anything except gobbling them down, and when my plate was empty I could see the empty time there would be between courses, since my parents eat so slowly. They push the gravy around the pieces of food, soak it up into their bread, and then stick the bread back in until it all gets absorbed. My father says that it's the best moment of the day. It's curious to think about a dinner table, about the hundreds of times there are the same people around it, and about the moments of real panic when they stop talking. I wondered what connected the three of us. I was losing track of who I was. I repeated "Anne," but the name on its own sounds hollow when you don't feel anything around it. Sometimes they talked about articles in the newspapers. Not political things, just accidents and crimes. It was sad. They saw things happen in the paper, even if they never saw them with their own eyes. My mother, who wanted so badly to have nice things, loved to plunge into the stories about bandits and criminals. Maybe it was out of a fear that they would kill us or steal from us. They would have been crazy to do that, seeing as how all our money was in the savings and loan. And then there were more accidents, and the kerfuffles at work, and people's illnesses. If those are really the only things in the world that seem important to them, I wouldn't want to live to be as old as they are. At meals, I noticed that deep down they didn't really like anyone, either in the neighborhood or elsewhere. There were a few people who were good but who had lost their way. They were set apart from the general wickedness. There was the neighbor woman with the laundry and the clingy kids. "She takes good care of her house." And then there was another person who was a real piece of work: Old Mrs. Collet. She was proud, and she believed in herself. They couldn't stand it that someone could believe in herself, especially when she came—let's not forget—from less than nothing. They always talked about individual people. There was never a word about the factory, or the school, or the institutions that the civics teacher had taught us about. Did they even realize they existed? Surely they did, but they didn't think they could talk about them. When they talked about compulsory military service, that conversation petered out right away. They said we have to have an army. "I'm telling you that a guy who doesn't do his military service isn't a real man. Why do you care, anyway? You're not going to have to do it." I persisted in asking my question: "But why do we need to have military service?" They got horribly angry and wouldn't answer me. I noticed, with disgust, that for them everything was just "the way it was." You could criticize *people*, but not other things. I liked it better when they didn't talk at all while they were eating. My time of the month came earlier than usual, so that kept me occupied. I had cramps, which was different from the other times, and I couldn't prevent my mother from finding out about it and telling me that it was normal. It seemed to me that it wouldn't have hurt so much if I hadn't been so bored. I stayed lying on my stomach all afternoon. My mother was very nice to me, giving me pills and one of her magazines to read. I thought about the year before, and then further back to other Julys, all the Julys of my life. It was hard to remember, but I noticed that for at least the last four years each year had seemed to be more separate from the year before. The steps were a bit higher, and on each step there was a girl, me, who was ugly and fairly stupid, except for today's step. I was happy that the steps were still rising. But maybe by next year I would think *this* year's girl was pathetic. That thought made me tired. And what about Gabrielle, that bitch who never came to see me? I never saw her in town, and it was impossible to go to her place. She would have thought I was chasing after her, and I had my pride. She reappeared one afternoon, wide-eyed with excitement. You can't imagine my happiness. That day really turned my head around. I thought that everything was finally going to change. My mother put on a good face for her. She makes up for it behind her back. "It's still such beautiful weather, Miss Gabrielle. Such a beautiful summer vacation." Weather is something old people like to talk about. It doesn't interest us. She tried to see if she could wheedle her way into the conversation. She always likes me to have friends, as long as she can "keep an eye on them." I thought about that while I was watching how close she stuck to us. She used to want me to mingle with the other little girls at the park on Rue Césarine. "Go play with them. Say hello to them. You go to the same school, don't you?" But that's not a good reason. It's horrible: you have to shake some girl's hand, even though you've never said hello to each other in all the time since you were little kids. You might look at each other, and that's enough, thinking, "You're here, and I'm here too." She would make me do it, and I would go home shamefaced afterward. And then there was Alberte. Seeing us together, she would

say, "If you were a boy and a girl you two would get married."
She must never have known about the dirty things we did
together, the poor woman. It's true that we kept quiet in front
of her, as embarrassed as a pair of fiancés, waiting for her to feel
like she was a third wheel and go back to her ironing. Gabrielle
and I moved away without rushing, so as not to arouse suspicion,
and we went into the yard near the currant trees and lay down
on bath towels. With all the dirty secrets that Alberte and I used
to whisper to each other, they would have put us into a juvenile
detention center on the spot. "Don't do anything that your
mother couldn't see you do," our elementary school teacher
told us. I knew Gabrielle had secrets to tell me. She hadn't
disappeared since the Saint-Pierre fair for no reason. She must
have had deep sources of strength to talk about blue jeans and
pullovers, and I must have, too, not to seem like I was curious
and in a rush to know everything. It's humiliating to have to ask
for details when you have nothing to offer in exchange. She
annoyed me by chewing on blades of grass with a superior look.
What was she waiting for? The real reason she had come was
to tell me about it. "I met a guy. He made me wait for a long
time, on purpose. He's a counselor at the summer camp, the
one they set up at the Point du Jour mansion . . . No . . . Yes."
It was like with Alberte: there had to be all kinds of playacting
before she would tell me anything. "You have to tell me!" "I
swear I didn't do it!" "If you swear it and you're lying, you'll
die. Didn't you know that?" "All right, I swear it on my parents'
heads." She made me drool with anticipation, since it was, you
might say, my own future that she was going to be telling me
about. I thought that everything that happens to other girls
would end up happening to me, just like getting your period. I
managed to act indifferent as she went on: "I rode on his motorcycle yesterday. We went for a ride together." She made me beg

again. There had been a field, and hay. She said, "You know, there are other counselors too: three or four of them." I didn't care about the rest of what she said. The only thing that mattered was the part about there being others. I asked, "What did you do together?" She put on her cat face again. "I can't say it, I can only whistle it." I felt so inferior to her. She ended up telling me about it anyway. My mother came and asked if we wanted a snack. She always tries to get in good with my friends. But young ladies have things to say to each other! We played innocent. The moment my mother left, I reminded Gabrielle about the other counselors, so that maybe . . . I would have liked to be even uglier than she was, so she wouldn't suspect anything. According to her, there were certain difficulties. "You're not as free as I am. And you would have to go on your bike." That was a mountain to climb. After she left, I felt discouraged, faced with all the problems you have to deal with when you're running after boys. The first problem, and the most difficult to resolve, is how to avoid anyone knowing about it. Then I saw the field, with the hay and Gabrielle's loosened breast spread out under Mathieu's hand. It's possible that I have no sense of decency, at least in my imagination. I would have gladly stolen the other hand for myself, fifty-fifty, one of us after the other. It's better to share than to have nothing at all. If Gabrielle really wanted us to be friends, then she had to make an effort for us to be in the same place with respect to boys. The gap between us was unacceptable. She already had too much of a lead on me. The fact that Alberte had been three years older than me, that I never caught up with her, still bothered me. With her boobs, her bras, the first shadows at the edge of her panties, and the little lump down below every month. She disappeared from my life before I even got to that point. I was jealous of Gabrielle. In any case, it was on that day that my vacation started to be less boring.

On the Sunday morning when the Tour de France was ending and my father was griping about the fact that the winner was a Belgian, they found my grandmother dead in her bed. She lived with my mother's sister on the other side of town. It was the first real thing that had happened since I finished middle school. My mother left the house, acting like a crazy person, and my father and I didn't see her again all morning. There hadn't been any deaths in the family for a long time. I had sometimes wondered how I would feel if my grandmother died. She was the only one left: the other grandparents had all died at the nursing home when I was a kid. There had been the funeral of an uncle. The house was full of people, but I went to school anyway—maybe it was elementary school—and I was happy to have some news to tell the other kids. The teacher scolded me, saying that it was sad and I shouldn't gossip about it, etc. But at home, no one seemed sad. I'm not sure, but I think they sang the drinking song "Boire un petit coup, c'est agréable," unless I'm confusing it with some other family dinner. So I thought about how the fact that she was dead made me feel, the fact that I would never see her again. It was hard. She had come to the house for the last time at the beginning of June, and my father had said to her, "Hey, grandma, it smells like someone's been farting. You know, you're going to kill us all." She didn't hear him because she was almost deaf, and I didn't think that was funny. I didn't feel that much when she died, but suddenly I was older. When I would think of myself as a little girl, it was sometimes with images of her, and now that she was dead something had slammed shut. We used to go to the cemetery, to my uncle's tomb, and my mother would tell me—"He's in heaven, and you know that he still sees everything"—and for a long time I was afraid that my grandmother would die, since she knew all the stupid things I had done. Since I no longer believed this, I felt only curiosity on the day of her death. It was kind of a funny day. I cleaned the kitchen for my mother, and I was happy. I was also thinking that I might be able to sneak away in the midst of the brouhaha, and that catastrophes could have a positive side. I was thinking about Gabrielle's boyfriends, and then about my grandmother, and the two things got mixed up, and it was a bit annoying because there was no relationship between them. I was thinking about who would logically die next after my grandmother. It would probably be my uncle Jean, although he was only fifty-eight. There was one memory I couldn't get rid of. I always saw my grandmother from the back, standing in front of her stove. She was making rabbit in cream sauce, and we were in the cellar playing with the rabbit skin and the cut-off feet, with pieces of blood still stuck to the hair. I was feeling happy, but also a bit wistful. My mother came back. I thought she would come back acting the way she said she was feeling earlier, but I was wrong. She didn't shed a single tear. She just sighed "it's over," with her eyes all shiny like Gabrielle's. At lunch, she told us that she was the one who had cleaned my grandmother up and put the rosary between her fingers. The priest thought it was perfect. I felt sick. My father said he would go and pay his last respects to my grandmother, and my mother said there was no need for me to go: "It's not a thing for young people." She was afraid that I would "take on sadness," the same expression my grandmother used when small children and young girls saw something they shouldn't have seen. That was fine with me. I preferred not to be reminded of my grandmother seen from the back with the smell of her melting butter for a roux. You would think there wasn't much to say about a sudden death, but my mother spent the whole next day talking about it with the neighbors. At times she told it like a crime novel: how she had found her, with her bowl of café au lait empty. "So she must have eaten breakfast and then gone back to bed. It's obvious! She was still warm, and she was lying there as if she was really asleep, with the sheet pulled up over her chin." People were expecting some kind of explanation, but there wasn't any. My mother was still going over all the details, and ending with, "I know we don't live forever, and at least she didn't suffer." Several times, when the neighbor came to get the details, she wiped her eyes dry with the kitchen towel she has holding. All that garbage exasperated me. I noticed that there was less and less of a relationship between the way I was feeling and what she was saying. I don't know if she loved my grandmother anymore, or at what age it becomes less painful to lose your mother, because it has to happen at some point. I told myself that when I'm forty-eight, the age of my mother, it would be easier. My mother must have been putting on a show. There was suddenly a lot of activity in the house, like on the day of my first communion when there were mattresses on the floor for the members of the extended family who slept over. Everyone thought I looked good in my new glasses. My grandmother was out of the picture. It was just an excuse for everyone to get together. There was a whirlwind before the funeral. I didn't go to the funeral: someone had to stay home and watch over the veal roast that we would be eating for lunch. And besides, the dresses I owned were too revealing, and my mother didn't think it was worth laying out the cost of a mourning outfit for me to wear to a funeral. My uncles and aunts talked about the same things my parents always talked about in the evening at dinner: work, rent, bills. They all talked at the same time, and they ate charcuterie. I thought they were even worse than my parents. My uncle Jean told about how a guy was crushed by scaffolding and was unrecognizable afterward. There were no cousins my age, just a twelve-year-old girl. I was sad that my aunt Monique wasn't there, because of my cousin Daniel who would have come with her. My mother started off, "You saw how no one budged from Monique's house. Believe me, when you don't have respect for your own parents you're not worth much. Not even flowers for her own mother's coffin!" Everyone got into it while they were eating the veal. "We may not be rich, but we have our dignity." They talked about Daniel, a real hothead who had already had—wait till you hear this!—thirty-six different jobs, and who had been in a fight at a dance. He came out of it pretty well. I remembered that he used to take correspondence classes in karate, or jujitsu, and I remember a book that he had about how to succeed at life in twenty lessons. He had lots of illusions. He was always trying to find shortcuts that didn't go anywhere, trying to score big with everything he did. At seventeen, he was kicked out of high school. When I was fourteen, I was in love with him. But I had come to see that it wasn't possible anymore, not with everything they threw at him. I had tears in my eyes. That happens to me now whenever I see bad things happening. You have the feeling that it's just bad luck, and that you can't do anything to change it. Daniel had really gotten off to a bad start in life. It scared me to think about that, to try to make sense of it. Does something like that just happen all of a sudden? How do you recognize the signs? Or is there one thing you do that takes you off the straight and narrow and makes you take a wrong turn? They were all saying that it was his parents' fault for not having disciplined Daniel enough. I was stupefied to see how they all agreed, how they all felt the same way about it. The funniest thing is that they started arguing about the details. Did Monique live on the Rue Eyries in Le Havre for eight years, or was it six years, or, no, wait a second, seven years? It took time for them to form an opinion so that the truth could come out. They got more and more lost in the details. By this point, my grandmother had been completely forgotten. Nothing they said interested me anymore, even though, as a kid, I had enjoyed family dinners: the platters of cake, the songs, the antics with the cousins in the kitchen. But when you're a kid you don't listen to the words people say, if you even hear them. They're just background noise. All I could think about was when I could get up from the table, and about Gabrielle and what a slut she was. And those grownups—it's crazy—they go around in circles searching for god knows what, talking about this and that and the thing they found at the supermarket, as if all those details were important, or as if they led somewhere. And the coffee, and the after-dinner liqueur, and then more liqueur. What was it that attached me to them? There was that gap between us again. Finally, they got up to stretch their legs in the yard. It was too late in the day, and the vegetables were covered by a patch of shadow. It was like the day of my exam: the afternoon had gone by without my noticing, but that didn't help with anything. There's nothing worse than the end of a dinner party. My uncles went out into the alley beyond the beans, and my aunts' dresses rubbed against their butts. It was ugly and old. Before, I used to love the days when there was a party for us and not for other people: in other words, when we were the privileged ones. But on the evening after the funeral, I was actually relieved when it was over. They all smothered me with kisses, saying, "Well, goodbye, Anne. Work hard in school. It'll be so great if you can become a schoolteacher." Like everyone else, I had eaten too much and drunk cherry liqueur. My parents said it wasn't worth making supper, since we were already full. It's always like that on the nights after a party. But I felt dirty and heavy. Also, I thought that I had wasted another day. Gabrielle was moving ahead, while I had to listen to my aunts compare the price of vegetables. If there hadn't been the burial and the dinner afterward, I wouldn't have been in such a hurry to . . . My grandmother had died at the right time. At seven o'clock it was still light out, and they weren't watching TV. Not on the day of the funeral, at least. They were putting things back in order, and during that time I ended my day in a bad way, no worse than the rest of the shitty day. At least I would be able to go to sleep afterward. I had less qualms about doing it in the evening. That way, if God existed and my grandmother could really see everything from up there, she wouldn't come back to tell people about what I wanted to do on the day of her burial, and what I did do, because once you have the idea you can't go backward. That was my way of burying her.

The next day, my mother was working at the Petite Vitesse. At two o'clock I showed up at Gabrielle's apartment building. While her mother was unpacking groceries, Gabrielle stirred her coffee around with a spoon. It made a scraping sound, which I hated. I would have been glad to do without our friendship if there had been another way of getting to know interesting boys. Anyway, I always thought that it was just temporary while I waited for something better. In elementary school, which wasn't coed, I changed certain girls into boys in my mind. I forgot to tell Gabrielle that my grandmother had died. I looked around Gabrielle's apartment, which had a simple décor like ours, but with completely different objects. It's weird to be in someone else's home, and even worse when it's the home of someone else's parents. I still liked my mother better than Gabrielle's mother. Other people's mothers are always disagreeable, and for a long time I wondered how it was my friends didn't realize that their mothers were ugly. With Gabrielle, what repulsed me the most was having to imagine the same intimacy between her and her mother as between me and mine. There was something maternal in Gabrielle's face, in her way of sitting diagonally on one but-tock, with one elbow on the Formica. She seemed bothered by my coming, just like I was. Her mother continued to take out tins of herring, and apple juice, which I hate. I wanted to get away from this scene as quickly as possible. I wanted us to be closer to equals again, like in school where it felt like we didn't have families. As for the teachers, they say "parents" in the same way they say "society" or "work," like it's something very vague that doesn't concern them. Gabrielle must have had an antenna about her mother, to know when we could and couldn't leave together. I had to wait. "Oh, you're here to go to the pool with me." Wink. "Wait while I get my swimsuit." Half an hour later we were on the highway, going in the opposite direction from the pool. I had taken off my top in the bicycle storage area of her apartment building so that I wouldn't have strap marks on my skin. I was planning to take my glasses off just before we got to the main building of the summer camp. It was better to keep them on for riding a bike, I thought superstitiously. What would happen if I fell on my face, seeing as my parents didn't know about my excursion? Yes, I was scared. It would have almost been a relief to me if someone had told me that the bike pedaled backward. But I had to do things I was afraid of. Otherwise, I would be better off staying home in the bosom of my family until the start of the school year. In other words, dying. I didn't know where I was heading, like in a romance novel. And even in *The Stranger*, I remember, there was the sentence, "And each successive shot was another loud, fateful rap on the door of my undoing." But I couldn't have thought about that then because I didn't suspect anything. Now, knowing what was going to happen next, everything is twisted around.

There were five of them on the lawn of the summer camp: five guys, that is, and two girls. I found out that they were waiting for the end of the little kids' nap. The calculations were made quickly. There were three guys left: the two girl camp counselors would already have paired up. Gabrielle had Mathieu, so I still had a choice between two guys. But which one to choose? Things were getting interesting. I was living. They were all pushing it to the limit with their dirty jokes and stories, and I would definitely have been uncomfortable except that I saw the two girl counselors listening and laughing calmly, and Gabrielle too, which proved that they found all this dirty talk to be natural. Their attitude reassured me, and I stopped blushing and even laughed at a song the boys were belting out, the girls accompanying with la la las. It was pretty. Sometimes I wanted to hum along, even though the words of the song didn't seem very funny to me. "Mommy, what's a virginity? It's a bird, my child, a bird that you put in a cage until it's fifteen years old." Gradually, I overcame my fear. At first, I thought they were all old and ugly. All of them were over eighteen, and people in groups always seem ugly to me. I got used to it, but I still couldn't see myself with any of them. A red-and-white dog was roaming around us. It seemed sick, and several times it went to do its business in the weeds. People even made jokes about it. I can't stop thinking about something kind of nasty that happened at that moment, before everything started. I was watching this dog and I didn't know that in September I would come back to this same lawn, and that just seeing the dried dog poo—which would no doubt disappear with the winter's rains—I would realize that something was over for the rest of my life. It was terrifying. So anyway, on the first day there was this sick dog. On the second day, my mother wasn't working at the Petite Vitesse, and I had to be more daring. "I'm going to Gabrielle's," I said, watching her face when I had pronounced this sentence. She wasn't suspicious. She just said, "Well—before, you never talked to her, and now you're glued together." I was careful. I kept a normal expression, a little sad, like I was saying

that I was going to Gabrielle's because I didn't know what else
to do. Also, I didn't want to show too much attachment to my
friend, or she would have been jealous. Getting my outfit wrong
would be unpardonable: there could be no question that I was
putting on something too low cut, or that my jeans were too
tight. I put up my hair, put a top on under my dress—the old
one—and left before she could see the darkness of my eyelashes
or the mauve of my eyelids. Above all, no perfume, which would
send up an alarm. I had to take the bike out calmly, since she was
surely watching me from the kitchen. I had to walk like a kid,
without fuss, hiding my chest and my butt as much as possible
so she wouldn't see any of the changes there had been in my
body since the previous year. I wore my glasses like I was proud
of them. I wanted her to be focused on the dangers of riding a
bike: "Pay attention, and stop at the stop signs." "Yes, I even get
off." "Good." As long as she's not worried about anything other
than the road, there's no danger. This time, sitting on the grass,
Gabrielle next to Mathieu, they talked about politics. I didn't
understand much of it, but I was happy. For once I was going to
learn something. I mean outside of school, where it's repellant
to always hear about things that you *have* to learn, and nothing
else—no dirty stories, just useful things. "Life will teach you,"
my parents say. That lets them off the hook of having to teach
me anything. I was listening, almost without thinking about the
fact that it was the boys who were doing all the talking, and that
in situations like these there are always hidden intentions behind
the words. Mathieu took the book that Gabrielle had brought. It
seemed that the author was a fascist. What did that mean? That
he was shafting the working class. I had read Gabrielle's book,
and I hadn't noticed anything. If what Mathieu was saying was
true, then the author in question, Guy des Cars, knew what he
was doing, since I really couldn't see what the problem was. I said

to Mathieu, "He never even *talks* about the workers." Point for me. "Exactly: that's the proof." Point for him. I never did know how to argue, but I didn't believe Mathieu at first. How could it be that no one had ever warned us about these books? Even my mother wasn't suspicious. In any case, it seemed exaggerated to say that there was a relationship between a sad little book and the work my father did at the factory. I was interested in politics and tried to keep up. At my house, we never talked about it. My father is in the union, but there's no politics in his union, and my mother is firm on having none of that in the house. Otherwise, there would be fights. I lost track of the discussion when they started talking about the Arabs and Israel, even though I thought I was pretty well caught up on the subject: the airplane hijackings, the hostages and the terrorists. I had been following it on TV because I was so bored during this summer vacation. That made me feel humiliated: I had the impression I had gotten everything completely backward, or else the guy on TV had been telling us lies. But I found the adventure exciting. I hadn't come expecting an argument, but I noticed that it spiced everything up. It even seemed like talking together helped us to make our choices, more in what lay underneath the words, and even sometimes in the look in people's eyes. You had to be really smart to guess which of the boys were already with the girl counselors, because I couldn't see any difference in the way they were looking at me. Nothing had changed since the first day.

In August, my father's vacation began. I always hate that. His vacation never works out, or maybe it's something about it being the month of August, with the heat. It's like one long Sunday, and they work up a sweat and become insufferable. Nothing ever happens. But I had found pretexts for going out in the afternoon. The pool with Gabrielle, shopping with Gabrielle, everything with Gabrielle. Unfortunately, I knew what she was up to in the evenings around six o'clock when I went home, and sometimes I looked at the shapes under her top, thinking about certain things that she must have let happen. This was the start of it all, or the day before the start, and I would have preferred it if I'd never had to move past this day. I had enough of songs and conversations on the grass, and of deciding what I was doing with these guys who were so much older than me. I didn't know what I wanted anymore. But my mother had a string of her bad evenings, talking about how the paint on the door was flaking off, or who is who, or how we can never have anything good without something or other. That eliminated any hesitation on my part. It made me feel like the only way I could punish her was by being loose. I don't think it serves any purpose to be sitting calmly between your parents, your legs under the table and your childhood behind you, when you're thinking about a path that goes toward a pasture that leads to an old bridge I could be leaning against, already covered by someone whose face is still indistinct. Nothing mattered, not even getting a zero in math. Maybe having a high school diploma matters. It's only from the point I'm at now that I can say that. There was only Mathieu and a kind of beanpole they called Ratty because he was all hairy. The girl counselors had good taste. Only the ugliest guy was left for me, and I could already imagine everything Gabrielle would say about him. I was the one who suggested going to the railway bridge, saying it was awesome. The path was wide open, but where would I be at the end of it? I couldn't hear the others anymore, and Mathieu was next to me. Panic. I wish I could still feel that fear of not being able to turn back. That's all over now. Too bad for Gabrielle: it's everyone for herself. It seems that you shouldn't let yourself be treated like an object, and yet they had swapped us behind our backs, like a pair of socks. It was Mathieu himself who told me that I had behaved like an object, but that was afterward. For me, that kind of thing had no importance. On the contrary. Ratty didn't do much for me, and anyway the first time there is too much hullabaloo going on inside for you to pay any attention to the face of the client. All of my childhood was like a trail of powder leading to this moment. I had certainly dreamed about it enough. There was one evening with Alberte when we kissed, turning off the lights of her bedroom, creating the illusion, but also a sense of anguish about what we were going to discover. Her lips were pinched and cold: she was as afraid as I was. I didn't feel anything. It's the only game of make-believe where you could never believe it was real. And those walks around the paved courtyard of the elementary school, and under the lime trees of the high school, where boys seemed like a dream that would take me out of the arms of girls, arms that are just like mine and that cling to me during recess. I wrote the names of the big girls I thought were beautiful on the walls of Rue Césarine. They were twelve years old, and I was seven. It was always a temporary solution, only temporary. If it hadn't been, maybe I wouldn't have been afraid to touch Alberte, and I would have enjoyed it. And everything they said, constantly, for ten years—first of all, that it was done with your finger, lightly, and that it was so easy—had to be interpreted liberally when you were dealing with men. The next step was seeing yourself nailed to the ground and having your image of something flat being replaced by that of a deep space you couldn't even see. But I didn't back away from anything, and little by little I patiently put together the puzzle of the different parts of the body and their uses. There were still a few blanks remaining. How fortunate that Alberte had a whole bag of jokes that were more graphic than a medical dictionary: "There's the smallest train station in France, my girl. Only a single traveler comes in, and the balls stay outside. Try and figure it out." The future was a big bed where you had your legs in the air for long stretches of time underneath very tender boys. I was about to soil all of these memories and leave behind my imaginary muddles, the slightly sticky world of girlfriends, being with Alberte when I was ten, the toolshed. And also doing things with my hands, which are still just a part of *me*. I was walking with Mathieu, but I didn't have anything planned, except for the parts with the lips and the arms, like in books and films. And then the fantasy gave way, as I felt the very real and rough skin of this boy, his watch pressing into my shoulder, and his smell. The actual reality of it is terrifying. I didn't know what to do, in any sense. I was really alone, Alberte. Gabrielle had gone off with the beanpole. They had taught me everything, but now there was nothing left other than me, breathing. Maybe you're always a spectator the first time. Why is it that the only thing you don't plan for is the brutality of boys, their lack of tenderness? All my dreams had been so wishy-washy. He was squeezing me too hard. It wasn't like anything I had read, either in the novels in my mother's magazines—"they embraced tempestuously"—or the poetry in the literature textbook—"one evening, do you remember, we sailed on in silence." I thought about my cousin Daniel, and then about the hall monitor I used to watch at the end of June. I suddenly saw all men. I held the great secret, even if on that day it was only a mouth and hands on my bra straps. I saw all the young men and the old men in the whole world, and myself as well, in the circle. It was all too simple to be a secret. From that afternoon on, I felt that I was on the same side as the grownups. But who is speaking, who is remembering, who is the Anne of that moment? Those are things that you only understand a long time afterward, when you are the Anne of today: in other words, no one. But, to continue. We sat on tree stumps that were by the side of the path and that were blurry because I didn't have my glasses on, and we started talking. We didn't talk about what we had just done, or about what we were still doing. We talked about how happy he was, and about the summer vacation, the camp, my skin, the trees that we shouldn't cut down, and Gabrielle—that interested me, what did he think of her?—and he touched my chest a little. I would never have thought that you could talk about unconnected stuff, both stupid stuff and serious stuff, with such freedom. I could see that to really talk, in confidence, you had to start by kissing and touching, and not the other way around. But he was the one who confided the most. I was quiet because he was older, because he had finished high school and other things, and because I had just let myself be kissed for the first time. It seemed very beautiful to have stolen him from Gabrielle. His very blue eyes, his long blond hair—at times, I was reminded of novels from *Today's Women*. I cried out, "If only my mother could see me." I used to laugh with Alberte and, putting my hand over my mouth, whisper the same thing. But now it was more of a cry of victory, first of all because she, poor thing, was waitressing at the Petite Vitesse, so there was no danger of her spying on me, and also because it showed that I had dared, that I was saying "screw you" to her. In short, it was a cry of amazement. He told me that I was being a kid to bring my mother into it, that I was free and the only one involved. He tried to unbutton my dress in the back. It was true what he said about being free, but it seemed to me that that could only apply to me later on, maybe when I was eighteen. Mathieu didn't realize that it would have meant coming home that evening, waltzing in and saying, "I'm going out after dinner. I don't know what time I'll be home. Give me the key." I can just imagine the looks on both of their faces. True freedom was not as simple as he proclaimed it to be, not at the age of fifteen and a half when you don't earn yet, as my father would say without specifying what, though it wasn't necessary to spell it out since for them it could only be money. The kids' naptime was ending, and we had to go back with Gabrielle and her guy. He pushed me up against a tree with his whole body. I suddenly stopped being a spectator. It was as if my body rose to my head. The words that we didn't dare to use because of their dirty meanings—"hard-on," "stroking"—came into my head, but they weren't shameful anymore. They became shameful again later on when I was telling Gabrielle about it and I didn't have a lot of other words to use. Gabrielle was trying to drag it out of me, saying, "I don't care what those pick-up artists do," with the result that I didn't say a single word to her the whole way home. I didn't want to break off relations with her, because I needed to be able to go out. Parents force us to find a way of doing it without raising any suspicion. That first time, when you go back to the house afterward, you can't really behave normally, opening the garden gate like you do on other days, acting as if today was like the evenings a few years ago when you were a kid. He had said "Anne," and I repeated it, "Anne." The nicest part is always what brings you back to things you have read or seen, to where someone said "Anne" in a certain voice, maybe in a film. I had to see my parents again. My mother lifted her head up from her sauce. I wished I could have slept somewhere else, at a friend's house, for a few days, so that I wouldn't have to hide everything from them. Why do you always have to go home? When I was in elementary school, one day after school I asked myself the question, "Why do I have to go back there and not somewhere else, to that family and not another?" My feet were walking on the sidewalk of Rue Césarine. "Is it because dogs and hens never get it wrong and I have to act like them? But still, why me and those people? Why are *they* my parents rather than other people?" I didn't know about giving birth, the blood, the breast milk, and everything that later on made me repress this question. Now it came back. If I could have told them everything, I wouldn't have had these strange ideas. My father was reading the *Paris-Normandie* newspaper. I went to my room and went over it all in my head. There was no longer the possibility of sharing him with Gabrielle. It's only in the imagination that you can cut a boy in two. "You get the top half and I get the bottom half, Alberte." At dinner, my mother ate a lot and she started complaining—"oh, my legs, my legs"— just to annoy my father while he was on vacation. She had wrinkles on her cheeks, and she looked very old to me at forty-eight. Because of my grandmother's death, she was still avoiding wearing light colors. It had been a long time since she and I had cuddled for pleasure. Now it was only out of obligation, when we had been separated for a long time, and since that almost never happened it had been three years since we'd embraced. Something else had also ended between my mother and me. How could I tell her? It was unimaginable. She brags about how serious she was, even when she was working in the factory. "I have my morals. I wouldn't have wanted to be called a piece of ass with no hands." That's what she said, and it made me laugh just to picture it. While getting undressed, I discovered a green stain on my dress. What a fuss they'd make if they saw it. I would have to be so careful about hiding all the signs, and put my glasses back on a hundred meters from the house.

I needed Gabrielle and me to be friends again. She, too, needed an alibi for her escapades to the Point du Jour summer camp. "If only you could go out at night," Mathieu implored. Impossible. We had to move faster. On another afternoon, when two or three days had passed in discussions and hesitations, we went to the railway bridge, under the tracks. Alberte said it was very green down there, full of hard snails the color of stones, and that you had to stay there bravely as a train went by. The world disappeared there. Alberte said that only abnormal people went walking there: a deaf mute with a rifle, a crazy person who should have been locked up. I didn't meet the deaf mute, and no train went by. I came back up with Mathieu into the light of an oat field. We walked just to have a break from our stops, and also because I was afraid to sit down and stay too long in the same place. But it was a field. Maybe I shouldn't have let it happen so fast. I never knew the code, the morality of it. For me, that would have had to be learned over many months, because my parents didn't teach me anything. Other girls might have more chances. They decide on what day to flirt, to have sex, and at what age, with what guy. That's definitely what I lacked, but why was there this difference? Mathieu said that everything was natural. I thought about an ad in a newspaper I saw when I was at the eye doctor's office: "The Lola bra removes the seducer's nightmare since it opens from the front." But it wasn't so natural. There was only about half an hour left. We always had to calculate because of the camp kids. I felt panic when he took my hand. What I felt was too intense. I thought about the public toilets, with writing all over them: "Titi is a fat ass-chaser." "Bébert's cock sticks up like a votive candle in church." There's nothing flaccid there. Every one of them is more erect than the last, a way of saying hello to girls who took risks. I couldn't pee in front of these enormous hieroglyphs. All these people obsessed with sex. That's an opinion I can only have from a distance. Up close, I didn't see Mathieu as someone who was obsessed by it. I never thought that, even on that day when I finally came to know the real size of what I had imperfectly imagined. "Mommy, what's a virginity?" I knew right away that it was the fear of this enormous thing. I suspected that once I had tamed it by seeing it and touching it, I might be capable of doing anything. When would I stop imagining myself being pierced through, massacred by this monstrous "thing" going into what I still thought of as a small and fragile place. "Don't touch it or you'll have babies." "The pussy is precious." But it was already shrinking in my hands, like the stupid balloons they used to have in shoe stores— and that reassured me. I told Gabrielle that I was crazy about him, since she had just admitted that she liked taking walks with Ratty. A two-way exchange. At the end of the first week, Mathieu asked me—his hair had fallen over his face, and he was very serious—"Is that how girls masturbate?" I was surprised that someone could ask me a question like that. It was basically what we were doing, but the words didn't seem right to me. There was something public toilet–like about it. And then afterward he said, "Don't tell me you've never fiddled with a girl. You're all halfway dykes." It was the first time I'd heard that word. I understood it, but I didn't like this kind of vocabulary, and I felt sad. I think it's better not to name things, or else to invent a name. Maybe boys don't have a lot of imagination, so they repeat the same words from one generation to the next. Alberte and I had lots of secret words: for men, we called it a "titite" or a "baisette," and for us girls it was a "carabi" or a "that thing." We inverted the genders in our choice of words. It was just games with Alberte—no expectations, no repercussions—and I didn't know how to explain to Mathieu why I had never been a dyke. I never felt panic with a girl, even when we were all alone in the toolshed. The panic is what distinguishes it. I should have been suspicious of him, of those expressions. It's always the dirtiest ones that stay in my head. On another day, I got up the courage to tell him that my father was a factory worker—not completely, since now he was a foreman—and that my mother had also been a factory worker. I told him that she had been waitressing at the Petite Vitesse for only a few years, and soon she would not need to work. It bothered me a little to tell him, even though I had already seen how he looked down on rich people. He had a funny smile on his face, and he started off on a frightening riff. What he was saying was new to me and complicated. He called it "alienation." At first, I got the meaning confused with either exile or craziness. So, it seemed that my parents were alienated, and of course they weren't aware of it. And they weren't the only ones. There were lots of people like that. It was reassuring in a sense. He treated me like an idiot, which I didn't think about as much as I should have. I wasn't angry. I was learning things, and that always made me keep my mouth shut. Mathieu became more patient and started again. "Your parents, you see, they're happy to have their house, even on credit, and that prevents them from wanting to talk about power, about responsibilities, about wanting to be free." I didn't dare to tell him that I wasn't really sure my father would want that: responsibility, or even freedom. They made me keep going with my studies so that I could be better than them and make more money, not for the sake of freedom. What would it take to change them? Mathieu was perfectly correct in his argument: you had to eat, and therefore you had to work. But there was no education going on at my house, and no money with which to be free all of a sudden, unless we turned into gypsies. If I talked like my parents, it was because I didn't know about anything else. My cousin Daniel, the hothead, was not a success. Mathieu forgot about the fact that each day we were supposed to be getting progressively closer to each other's bodies. He said we had to fight for a change in society. I, too, like the idea of revolution. The only interesting period in history was Joan of Arc getting burned at the stake, and I don't see the point of constitutions. When I was a child, I dreamed about the end of the world, about being able to gather up everything that was in the shop windows, especially cakes and chocolates, and sleeping in the beautiful showroom bedrooms on display at the furniture stores on the Rue de Calvaire. I drooled when my mother told me about how people had pillaged stores during World War II: not criminals, but people like us. "But during wars, you lose all your moral sense," my father added. I would have liked to lose that. But it seemed that all this—filling your shopping cart to the brim, beautiful bedrooms, or paid vacations in the sun—was still not true happiness. Mathieu was determined. It was also difficult for me to imagine real freedom when I didn't even know what it looked like. I thought about love, about the oat field that was very far from my parents, with thoughts of school hardly existing anymore. Yes, I finally understood. You should make love: it's unhealthy to be a virgin. I liked to listen to Mathieu. It was the most beautiful two weeks of summer vacation in my whole life—even when I wasn't going to the summer camp and was mildewing at the house—because I was asking myself questions. All these people at the supermarket, or in their cars, who didn't know they had missed out on their lives. I felt superior to them for knowing. It was something that would only help me out later, because for the time being, as I was watching my parents smother the tender green beans they had grown in the garden with sauce—"that's one more that no one will steal from us," as my father liked to say as he stretched after eating—I didn't know how I could make them see that they were exploited and unhappy without even realizing it. Mathieu had talked to me about the masses for a long time, but in the evening in front of the TV, his story didn't seem very real. People were one at a time. The mass was abstract. Taking everything, breaking things, fist in the air with cheeks striped by sunlight, all bathed in red: none of that fit when I looked at my parents. First of all, they never want to ask for anything in person. If they need an authorization for something, they undermine themselves by speaking politely. Maybe that's how they get taken advantage of. My father always took one glass of booze—well measured—never more. I'm the one who was unhappy about their alienation. They watched a magician's trick on TV, where some country bumpkins were coming up and getting asked about their reactions and about the type of show, taking on elegant manners and pretending not to understand anything—"What do you mean? Could you repeat that?" Proud to be on TV, these people couldn't see that they were being made fun of. I said, "This show is stupid. Let's watch something else. This magician is treating people like idiots, but we don't have to feel sorry for them. If they go on the show, it's because they want to. We wouldn't do it." I tried to say more, but they weren't even listening. "Stop talking, you're making it hard to follow." They had been my parents for too long: I could never give them a political education. What would Mathieu have said in my place? But they weren't *his* parents. I would have liked to be out all the time, walking the whole morning until Gabrielle came on her bike to pick me up. I did every possible kind of errand to get out of the house without raising suspicion. Going out for the sake of going out was too shady. I stopped saying hello to the women who took their time before answering. Definitely prostitutes. It was easier to murmur a vague hello that stays in the throat. My father, working in his garden, didn't think anything of it when I went out on my bike. Fathers who think boys are always bastards put themselves in the place of the guys who are going out with their daughter. And my mother, who watched over me like a hawk, didn't see any danger. She used to wash out my privates when she was alone with me. "You mustn't let anyone touch you, Anne. Tell me if anyone does." "Touch"—what a joke. It's not the touching that's bad, it's the pleasure you take from it. You understand that pretty quickly. You would have to touch it and not feel pleasure. Alberte said that her mother said that women never like it, and on the swing set I swore that I *would* like it, even if that wasn't normal. It started off well: touching myself was a pleasure, as my crafty mother suspected when I was only five. When I left on my bike that afternoon of August 14—I'm always leafing through the calendar, but it doesn't explain anything to say it was Saint Eberhard's Day or that the sun rose at 4:44 and set at 7:06, and the horoscope is now long gone—it was something I was doing for myself, alone. I rode the three kilometers along the national highway, earlier than usual and without Gabrielle. My parents had left for Le Havre at one o'clock. "You have to take advantage of vacations." The timing was perfect: Mathieu had his day off. He must have engineered the whole thing: his motorcycle, the route he chose. If I had suspected what we were about to do, it's hard to know if I would have agreed. And it's my own fault. I heard my father saying, "the man proposes, the woman disposes," and later on Mathieu would say, with a smart-aleck look, "the woman gives herself and the man loans himself." But those aren't the right words either. I don't understand them. I'm still here, entirely complete: I get hungry, I urinate, I sleep, I look at myself naked. I didn't give myself, and he didn't take much, and it was so badly done. That's not the problem. I don't know the meaning of that day, except that I was sure that we couldn't start touching each other, even the tips of our fingers, without wanting to go the whole way. I had never been on a motorcycle before, feeling the wind, wearing the helmet. No one would have recognized me there, my body so light compared with the big fatty I felt myself to be. I was afraid of dying and my parents saying, "What was she doing there, on the road to Veules-les-Roses?" That really could have happened, because they didn't know. Or maybe there would be a breakdown and I would come home late at night, half frozen. The road was safe: it had been more than a month since there had been a drop of rain. That also made me let go of my resistance. My body would have melted in the ambient air, if only I had the feeling that it belonged to me. The roofs abutting the sea appeared, and the open cliffs on either side. Until now, I had only gone to Veules-les-Roses with my parents, on Sundays in summer. We would eat hard-boiled eggs on the beach and my father would sleep under a towel. Sometimes cousins came too, like Daniel, and my mother would hide me while I peed at the foot of a cliff. We came down gently to the beach on the motorcycle, and we swam. I tried not to look at all of him, because he was in a very skimpy swimsuit, but I couldn't help it because I found it strange that we were displaying ourselves almost naked in front of everyone. We left pretty quickly. He didn't like this atmosphere of tanning, casinos, and advertising jingles. But it would have made me happy if we had run into some girls from middle school. We had a drink at a dive along the road, in Héricourt. Some guys were ogling us and making remarks. They might have been addressing them to us. "Hey there, I hope you've already made him shoot his wad." Personally, I've never been afraid of people horsing around. Their faces were bloated with laughter. One of them stayed quiet, while the other one got even more excited. "It's just that I would be glad to give it to your girlfriend." Mathieu found all this very fine, natural. It was strange to hear them. It seemed to me that the two of us were already playing in a farce, and it also seemed like there were no more of those old creeps left, those sex maniacs like the old geezer who told Alberte and me he wanted to give us a kiss on the eye. Suddenly it started to feel like everyone was bathed in it. There were no distinctions between the old, the ugly, or even the woman who was peeling beans on a table in the café. My parents did it too, though that still disgusts me. The Coca-Cola was getting warm. I had to be back by six o'clock. There was an hour and a half left. I knew what had to happen next, the yes-no: there is always this game between the two people involved. The motorcycle didn't break down, I didn't fall off, and I was careful not to get a grass stain on my red dress. It's too hard to get those out. My wet swimsuit was rolled up in a plastic bag. I just had diluted blood on my nylon underpants going home. I had imagined that it would be like the rest, very gentle. But it was like a dagger. I read that somewhere. Those descriptions have always interested me. I could almost quote from all the books I've read where they talk about it. And for one hour I squeezed my teeth together to hold back the tears. I dreamed about anesthesia, about fighting with I didn't know what. I felt humiliated. Maybe I hadn't waited long enough. Maybe I was still too afraid of it, of the immensity of it. I almost pulled back, saying, "No, let's do it another time, and then I'll be more prepared." I felt ridiculous, and he grumbled that I was a strange one and that he was going to break up with me. He was joking, of course, but it wasn't all that obvious. Alberte had said, "I want the first time to be in the ocean, in the water, but especially in the ocean, so that I won't have to feel it in me: it will just slide in without me feeling it." When he had succeeded in doing it, I felt a brutal emptiness. I had always wondered what it would feel like inside. It felt like nothing. I didn't even know where the tunnel ended. My mother wanted me to get my ears pierced, and I never wanted to. It's a medical procedure. You have to be insane to say that it feels good or bad. When you feel like crying out in pain, that's not the kind of question you ask. It was the first time I dared to look at his sex in broad daylight. I kept my panties at the bottom of the chest of drawers in my bedroom, and now I take them out sometimes because they're a symbol, like the fourteenth of August on a calendar, but more personal than a calendar. There's still the acid smell of old laundry on them. Looking at them, I don't know what they represent anymore. It's just a pink and yellow pattern on some cloth. It makes me think about the copy of the head of Christ on a sheet, a thing with faded, graying blood that I used to see at my grandmother's house and that scared me. I act like there was a before and an after. "Mommy, what's a virginity?" It's not a bird, or anything. It's certainly not the punctured skin that makes the difference. Instead, it was all the thoughts I couldn't stop having after I left him, on my bike and then at home, where my parents had not yet arrived at seven o'clock. I said to myself that theoretically I could die now, since I knew everything. I would have to live with that knowledge forever now. It was, in fact, something very ordinary. The time of my being able to dream about how it would happen was over. How can people crowd in front of porno movie theaters in Le Havre? Before, I used to ogle the posters. Not anymore. I took the cat onto my bed. She was already pregnant, according to my father, who had an eye for those things. It seemed to me that it hadn't really gone the way it was supposed to. If there hadn't been all the ridiculous and sad gymnastics, I would have liked Mathieu. I liked the image of him covered in sweat. I couldn't put my finger on exactly when the change took place. When we parted, he put his hand on me over my dress and said, "That's mine now." But it seemed to me that it didn't belong to anyone. I had already lost my nice, ignorant pussy eight years ago. It had been such a little, hidden creature. I didn't know what it wanted. It's called "purity." Easy to say. I don't have anything to replace it with yet. My mother gave it a funny name: she called it her "crougnougnous." It was an unnamable object. Ugh! I didn't have one of *those* in me! And then I thought that it was really none of my parents' business, and suddenly I wasn't afraid anymore.

I thought about those girls who go off on the arm of a boy and then get married because they're pregnant. Alberte and I used to wonder where they could have managed to do it. Now I had done it too. I was proud. And now I could put in a Tampax. I wanted to tell someone about it, to write about it, but I didn't know where to start because you always have to go so far back: to Gabrielle, to the middle school exam, and even before that, to the dream. I would have to tell it from way back in the past right up to today, but I would have to change my name. That would be more convenient. I would have to write it in the past tense because it sounds better, and that way I would be able to say everything under cover. I looked for a good first name— Arielle, Ariane, or Ania—where the first letter of the name would be the same as mine. But with a beautiful name like that, it wouldn't be me anymore. Stories about other people didn't interest me that night, so I wrote out a sentence, the kind you invent as you're writing: "I would like to leave." And then I crossed it out. It's not something you can talk about seriously, or else. I put on some records, but I didn't pay much attention to them. I would have liked to be able to play an instrument, the guitar for example, but my parents never wanted me to. "What's the point? You'd never have enough time to study." They didn't get home until around eight o'clock because of traffic, and that was all they wanted to talk about, especially since they were really, really tired. I was very happy that they had a subject of conversation. The next day, we had to put together the traditional meal for Assumption Day, August 15, when I would much rather have gone over to Gabrielle's place so that I could tell her about it. And then go see him again. They had invited my uncle Jean and his wife, of course, and their daughter, my twelve-year-old cousin, who had already come for the funeral. We have nothing to say to each other, since she's just a kid. In the middle of the meal, I fell into my frightening hole, where they all turn into talking, guzzling jugs. Maybe they think I like having my butt sitting on a chair for three hours like they do, listening to stories about the supermarket—this thing or that wasn't too expensive, and, "Anne, what do you have to say? You're not a very talkative girl!" What if I was like them, only eating, drinking, and driving around. This family puts me to sleep. Their lives are boring, and I had the feeling they wanted youth around them just to stop them from getting older. My little cousin got up from the table. She was allowed to come back just for dessert. If only I could have done the same thing: go eat a yogurt in my bedroom or at the far end of the yard, and dream. There were stains on the beautiful tablecloth, and bits of chicken on the edges of plates. I always start to go crazy during meals with the extended family. They suffocate me. They didn't want to see anything, whereas I, like Mathieu and every other young person, knew that life is contained in the gestures that people hide. One day, laughing, my mother said to a pair of newlyweds, "Hurry up and get laid!" For my parents, it was something to be gotten over with quickly, a kind of disposable item that wasn't worth as much as money or a good job. That had been enlightening to me. She didn't want me to run around, because of my studies. Everything would fall apart, along with her hopes for me. Maybe it was because I was on vacation, but I was convinced that I would do well in high school, and that nothing would fall apart. On the contrary: now that I had made love, I would have one less thing to worry about. "Have some green beans: they don't make you fat." What was happiness for them? Eating, more eating, buying things, TV in the evenings or else perusing the newspaper, and getting a good night's sleep. Mathieu had been right all along: they were alienated up to their gullets. But if it was me, I would rather not have to think about their kind of happiness. It was enough for me just to imagine that if a misfortune were to happen to me, they would be over-whelmed by sadness. But I would take care of it myself. I wouldn't set foot in the hospital. I'd deal with it right away, cut it right out. They all felt so far away from me. It was on that day, sitting at the dinner table, that I remembered a story from *Intimité*, which my mother loves because it's based on true-life stories. A girl runs away from home, lives somewhere—flat broke—and then comes back home. When her parents hear a baby crying in the room, they forgive her. That really got me confused. What was the connection between having sex with Mathieu and not being able to be a schoolteacher or an executive secretary? It seems to me that in my parents' minds there can only be one or the other. I, too, would like to be better than them: you'd have to be crazy to want to live like they do. She never really says it, but we all understand that it's lousy to be a manual worker. Sometimes I want to say to people who come to our house, like she does, "Don't pay any attention to the house." How can anyone say it's bad to want to lift yourself up? It's funny. All it takes is for me to spend a little time in the same environment as my parents and the rest of my family, hearing them talk, seeing my mother running from the kitchen to the dining room, looking heavy, her skirt curling upward at the bottom because of the wrinkle she always makes in it when she sits down, or seeing my uncle Jean, who is always smiling for no reason. He's proud of me, so I don't know who's right anymore. Everything gets muddled up when I'm with them, just like Mathieu said. I couldn't take any more of being at the dinner table that Sunday the fifteenth of August. How did the others do it? It seems to me that you would have to be a bit out of synch with your family after you've been down the garden path—and not looking for strawberries. I remembered the old guys making remarks at the café in Héricourt, at this same time the day before, and then "it" happening, and then the emptiness in the pit of my stomach. All of those things existed, but I didn't see the connection between them. If there *is* one, I still haven't figured it out. "Have one for the road, Jean. It's not the fifteenth of August every day!" "What have you been doing with yourself, Anne?" "She's been resting." "That's the best thing for her. Studies are tiring. You have to give yourself a rest if you want to achieve anything." What Anne were they talking about? That evening my uncle and my aunt stayed longer so they could all eat the leftovers together. That's what they usually do, as if they can't bear to leave each other. The same conversations, with the same pieces of chicken—only cold this time—on the plate. And my twelve-year-old cousin, innocent and no doubt wanting me to teach her things. But she's a kid. I'm done with my childhood now, and as a result I'm done with other people's childhoods. After a day like this, I decided that I had to do it again as soon as possible. Mainly because I missed feeling pleasure.

The next day, Gabrielle, the old hag, was waiting for me at the bottom of her apartment complex, on a grassy area that was baked by the sun. That was good, because we really needed to be friends for me to tolerate her little mouth saying, "You should have made your boyfriend wait longer." That made me wish I hadn't told her everything, even though it was mostly just medical and technical things, which are not that interesting. I was waiting for her to pay me back, so that the two of us could share our experiences. She had said that if I did it she would do it. "Oh, nothing special. I'm going with Ratty. He's a good guy, you know." She was lying, the slut, the old lynx with her bike racer's legs. But if I had left her alone on her lawn to think about what a coward she was, I wouldn't have had anyone to talk to. It seemed I had always invented the duties of friendship, trust and all the rest. You just had to look at Gabrielle—perfectly happy to know everything about me and keep quiet about herself—to understand that these lofty sentiments are just a pose. It might have been possible with Céline, but she didn't have a mind that was dirty enough for us to relate to each other. I would never have survived. Alberte had been the only one I could do that with, and even with her everything almost went sour one afternoon when my cousin Daniel tripped her while she was running. While he was helping her up, he placed his two hands like a fan over her budding tits. She said, "I laughed so hard that I almost peed in my pants." Those two very well-placed hands always remained between us, even if we never said anything. With Gabrielle, it was different.

The summer camp was going to end on August 30, and the counselors would be leaving. When you're not limited by time, when you have a whole year in front of you, you're able to think about things. I thought that maybe I would die at the end of summer vacation. Have a bike accident. During the kids' nap, we found a way for me to go up to Mathieu's room without the camp director noticing. I didn't say "if only my mother could see me" anymore because I didn't see *her* anymore. Sometimes I was afraid that I would forget what time it was and stay out until nighttime. That would have been a really bad thing to do. But it was impossible: deep down, I wasn't that careless. I'd gotten used to the empty space inside my body. Actually, that didn't play a big role in how well the sex turned out, but I didn't dare say that to Mathieu, because it would have bothered him. I told myself that it was only fair: if pleasure was to be found only in the part of you that was deep inside, girls would never desire it until they had been penetrated by a man, which seemed absurd and immoral to me. As I was leaving the Point du Jour, I hung out with Mathieu and his camp kids for a while. They were shouting, "That's your girlfriend," followed by a victorious "Yes!" I don't usually like kids: they're still too close to my age. But at that moment, as I started watching them play dodgeball and sing "We are the children of summer," it was as if they and I were in the same circle. They seemed so happy, even the losers, with their big eyes and the snot dripping from their noses. I envied the girl counselors. I would have liked to stay there with Mathieu and the kids. In that moment, I felt a great love for the whole world, especially for the disadvantaged. What a word. "The ones who don't have a penny to their name," as my parents say. The dirt poor. Maybe I was feeling superior because I had had sex with a fairly good-looking guy. But it was mostly because I felt close to them, to the kids, and even to old people. When I was little, I was terrified of dirty old men and of old women and their disgusting ways. Now, that was over. When I looked closely, there was no relationship between their decrepit bodies, the villainous look in their eyes, and what I had just discovered. There was also no relationship between my happiness and things like the dictionary definitions I had based my ideas on when I was twelve. It's hard to define why I was so happy. You can always talk about your actions, but it's harder to talk about your pleasure. It's like a secret. One afternoon, I sat down near the window of his room and watched him smoke on his bed, with the sunlight streaming through and cutting across his stomach. I decided that I would keep a journal. I would describe his room, and maybe his sex, using different words. We listened to Jimi Hendrix. I had never experienced the present moment so strongly. If that was what it meant to be sixteen, with days that were so full you could scream about it, then I was happy to be sixteen. Suddenly, my whole childhood had meaning, since it had led up to this point. During one October school break, I had been playing hide-and-seek at my grandmother's. I waited among the nettles behind the house for someone to find me, and they forgot all about me. The silence around me was full and strange. "I am Anne, Anne, A . . . nne, with the future in front of me, living until that future." I went to join the others. It was as if I had seen the Holy Virgin or some other saint who showed herself to me in a cloud. And now I was finally there. There was a feeling of harmony. When I talked to him and the other camp counselors, they taught me lots of words that I hadn't known before—"not too shabby," "bamboozled," "policing"—and I started to get a clearer understanding of the differences between the Right and the Left, between anarchists and communists. I think I would still get confused about it now, although it doesn't matter to me anymore. Since I haven't been around them, it would all be a fog. My parents aren't anything politically, and the teachers would light themselves on fire before they would announce their true colors. It seems that they aren't even allowed to. It would be really useful, though. Then we would know what the relationship is between their political ideas and what they tell us. Otherwise, you have to guess. When I heard Mathieu talk, I thought that the things he said were completely correct and intelligent, except for a few details which annoyed me, but that was probably because I hadn't really understood them yet. He claimed that everything depends on the education of the masses. He was right, and when I saw the kids scurrying around the summer camp I wanted to be a teacher for real, not just because it was a good career. But there was no way I could grasp the word "masses." In our family, and in the neighborhood where I live, we had always thumbed our noses at rich people. That didn't seem much like "the masses" in my book. To understand that word, I would have to think of a sad gray block with me in the middle: that idea of a mass. I also learned about responsibility and freedom. Those words seemed very real, especially since it was the summer and we didn't wear a lot of clothes in the heat. Going home was like going back to a stable. "God, please don't let them find out what I'm doing." What could I have gotten my parents to understand? Why the leftists are breaking shop windows and won't back down? They talk about the weather, the garden, and the number of cars on the roads. How does the revolution fit into all that? Other people would have to do it for them, and they still wouldn't agree. My father would ask what *he* got out of it. Things wouldn't be like they were before. In any case, I didn't want the revolution for them, since when I imagine a revolution I never see them as part of it. Mathieu also said that I should never forget that I was part of the working class, that it was important. At first I was almost ashamed of that, and what amazed me was that I had always been surrounded by it, all the while not noticing anything in particular. "That's because you can't compare yourself with middle-class people. Do you even know any?" I couldn't say I really knew any. I did say good morning and good evening to them: the eye doctor for example. Teachers are different: we don't know what side to put them on. One afternoon, when we were all together, we made a big ruckus in the village near the summer camp. We sang songs like "It's a bird, my child" in front of an audience of country bumpkins. I yelled louder than anyone else. I was happy to show off my freedom in front of people who looked like my parents. They were just as suspicious, but there was less risk. It had been more than a week, and I wondered how it was that my parents hadn't noticed anything in my behavior, or in the way I was coming home late sometimes. I couldn't even say how they were spending their days, except that my mother went to the Petite Vitesse from time to time. I kept track of her. That's how you realize how immobile your parents are. Maybe they didn't suspect anything because they were walking around with their noses in the air about what they were making me into. That made them blind to everything else, or else it just took more time for them to become aware of it. There were nine days left.

We got together to celebrate the birthday of one of the girl counselors, the one I liked more because she was laid back. I didn't know who she was sleeping with, so she was kind of mysterious. I wanted to be her when I was twenty. I've always looked at older women, grown-up women, and said, "I'll be like that." When you really think about that, it's impossible, and yet I still think about it a lot. It's too frightening to think that you're not like anyone else. We drank a lot of sparkling wine and we sang kids' rounds, and then a few "impolite" songs, as Alberte and I used to say. It was basically the same as the other time, just for fun. And Yan was there, sitting across from me. He wasn't with anyone. He was playing the guitar. Later, I could never understand how he managed to fool me with the way he talked, his boyish mystery. The idea that we could just be friends was all just froth, a bluff. I was already feeling bad about something that I thought would never happen. We sang the children's song "There's a roll, there's a pitch," with Yan holding me around the waist from the right side and Mathieu holding me from the left. The song felt far away, and something happened down below, inside me. On the right side of me, I felt that sense of panic again. I thought that Yan had fondled me. There should have been a moral battle. I could've at least played a game of heads or tails to decide. Instead, I sang with my throat tightened in anticipation, as if it had already happened. I had too much of a tendency to believe that you could only talk to someone after you had touched each other. It's impossible to do that in modern life, but I still thought about it that way. And then there was Mathieu, Mathieu who had disappeared from view. In that month of August, the past didn't weigh very heavily compared with the future. Curiosity is normal at my age: it would be strange if that wasn't the case. Except that for girls, curiosity can lead to anything, and it's frowned upon. These days I'm less and less curious: everything has dried up inside me. I was still imagining that things would proceed very slowly. What a joke! It was almost six o'clock, the time when the camp kids had their dinner. He was in a hurry. We went out into the oat field. That troubled me, since it was the same place where I had been with the other guy. Being in the wrong place makes you have bad thoughts about yourself. That oat field was both time passing and time not passing. He didn't talk much, though in the beginning it wasn't really necessary. But the beginning didn't last for more than five minutes. My excitement didn't rise to the level of his, and he wasn't even aware of it. I understood that he acted in a brutal way because he was following in someone else's footsteps, so to speak, and he must have been thinking about that the whole time. I didn't ask myself about the girls he must have had before. He left it vague. I felt that he would never see me as anything other than a slut. "Hey, will you come see me in my room?" I said no. On the way back, he told me that the girl counselor I admired so much was his girlfriend, and that it would be better if she didn't find out anything. And then he said, "Well, it really wasn't such a big deal anyway." For the first time, there was actually a divide between boys and me. Until then, it had always seemed to me that we were basically the same. But something had obviously escaped me, at least in terms of these kinds of moments. I protested, almost screaming at him, that he had no right to say that. When I feel a way that I can't explain, I scream out that people have no right. That expression sums it up for me. Yan moralized, "If you don't want people to treat you like that, you shouldn't act like an object that gets passed around." Suddenly, everything was clear. I felt sorry about everything I'd done, and I felt that Mathieu might have the same reaction and would send me packing. But I still thought that I could make up for everything. Riding my bike home, I wished it was already the next day so that I could know whether Mathieu was going to ignore me, or if I could convince him that Yan didn't mean anything to me. Since Mathieu had also left Gabrielle, maybe he wouldn't dare to blame me. Even Yan had cheated on his girl. When I thought about it, I hadn't really felt like an object. Or maybe Mathieu had also treated me as an object, even though from what I could see he didn't seem to suspect that was the case at all. But just remembering his smugness brought all my lofty reasoning back down to earth. Logic is worthless compared with the self-assurance of boys. When I got home, there had been a serious falling out between my parents. I immediately thought it was because of me. But no, they had gotten a dent in the car while they were out running errands. "You didn't see it when we got there? You can see it pretty clearly, can't you?" "The car is all your father thinks about. Me, I have other things to think about." Oh well: the summer vacation rarely goes by without a ruckus of some kind, which is only natural. I hadn't ever talked to Mathieu about it, but I'd known what these nights were like ever since I was really little. They would fight, and the police would come, and I would plug my ears. These days I'm less sensitive. That evening I was almost happy it had happened, since it spared me from having to talk. Besides, this wasn't the moment to stick my nose into things. They never seemed to think that hearing their fights might have an effect on me. When they do their song and dance about the stupid car, and I'm in the house with them, I feel like I'm suffocating. In the car, there's the smell of the fake leather seats as they stare silently at the road, like ugly statues. When they fight, they grab at each other's privates. I would have liked to turn the clock back by four hours. I washed my face and my chest. I didn't really believe that the cleansing powers of water were that strong, but it's instinctual to wash when you want to clean someone off you. "God, please don't let Mathieu find out." My body looked ugly to me for the first time during the whole summer vacation. I turned on the radio. They were playing the song "J'attendrai le jour et la nuit." Not a great omen. We ate, and my parents were quiet except for my mother abruptly saying she wasn't sure she was ready to go to Le Havre. I helped with the dishes, and I couldn't stop inventing a tomorrow when I would explain everything to Mathieu—that is, if Yan hadn't already said something. Or maybe even if he had. How could I stop Mathieu from knowing that I had wanted to do it. Even my breasts looked different. I looked at myself in horror. Do boys ever look at themselves in the mirror and say they feel horror? I cried into my pillow so that my parents wouldn't hear, especially my father, who has the knack of immediately asking me what's wrong. It's brutal. It always means "you're bothering us by not being happy."

The next day I went to find Gabrielle, because I wasn't feeling all that calm about going to the camp. "Promise that you'll help me. Act like I'm still going with Mathieu. I'll owe you one." In the hallway, we ran into Yan. I said hello, acting calm and smiley. I was disappointed when he answered, in a hurried way, "Hi, I'm taking the kids on a treasure hunt." Mathieu came out of his room, and Gabrielle yelled out really loudly, "Okay, I'll be leaving now. See you later." I could see from the serious look on Mathieu's face that he knew everything. "We can talk about what happened yesterday, if you want." Talking about it didn't take long. "If you wanted more of it, you should have said so." I was prepared for everything except crudeness, and I couldn't get him to move beyond that. He lay down on his bed, his arms tucked under his neck. "I'm not an asshole. If that's what you wanted, you got the wrong guy." It wasn't possible to have a discussion with him, so I sat down next to him, and I said some things that were a bit fake, a bit cheesy. We weren't used to saying things like, "You're the only one I belong to." He turned red, with his hair standing on end, and without a word he took his clothes off: just the bottom half. He wanted to pull off the jeans that I had put on that afternoon. I felt sick to my stomach. I would have liked to be dead. I took his hand off me. I thought about prostitutes. I used to talk about them all the time with Alberte, pretending it was something we wanted to do. I had stains on my jeans. He took the rest of his clothes off, kneeling on the bed, his legs spread a bit apart. Suddenly I felt far away from what was happening. Nothing had meaning anymore. "You're a cocktease," he said. He thought like Yan, and Yan thought like him. That way of thinking stretched to infinity, with me, like a turd, in the middle. I ran to the bathroom at the end of the hall. Music was coming out of the girl counselors' rooms, and it tore me apart to think about how harmonious their lives were. I cried over the toilet for a long time, and then I washed the stains off my jeans. In elementary school, a girl had gone to the bathroom in her underpants. She tried to hide it, and then during recess she stayed in the washroom for ten minutes. We laughed so hard. I didn't dare come out of my hiding place. I had gotten myself soaked while I was cleaning myself off. And Gabrielle, with her all-seeing eyes, would definitely have noticed it. There was always music around those girl counselors. That was the worst thing. I looked out through the doorway and saw that there was no one in the corridor. I left. I knew that I wouldn't want to see Gabrielle again. Afterward, on my bike, I rode any which way. I wished that some driver would hit me from behind so that I would feel nothing and it would all be over. The most atrocious thing was that when I was with them I had thought I caught a glimpse of freedom. They said it was unhealthy to be a virgin, and that society is there to destroy us. I did see freedom one day: the bed bathed in sunlight, the same bed as on this day. But that kind of freedom is worthless. They had rules, too, but I hadn't known what they were. As I rode my bike home, I whined to myself. It was too unfair to be excluded from a code you didn't even know exists. Could something like that happen to a boy? Relentless girls who would humiliate him enough to drive him crazy? I couldn't imagine it. I had started to think that I was lacking a code, a set of rules: not the ones made by my parents or by school, but rules for what to do with my body. There must have been rules about what was and what wasn't allowed. That would be practical in the case of someone who preferred the forbidden fruit. It would allow them to make their choice. Especially if you're just a girl. How could I have guessed that boys think and feel things so differently from the way I do? They all disgusted me. I remembered my hands, in the yellow sink of the bathroom, trying to clean my jeans, which were all dripping with "that." The cars were driving along the national highway, some of them honking at me as they went by. Assholes! My jeans were dry from the sun, so I could go back to my house. If it had been possible to go anywhere else . . . But where would I have gone? It was always the same problem. Near the front gate, I realized that I hadn't put my glasses back on. They were pushed into the pocket of my top. One of the lenses was broken. I remembered how I'd struggled on the bed. What a disaster. And now I would have to deal with this disaster. That was all I was thinking about. I went into the living room with my glasses in my hand. My mother was wearing one of my father's sweaters. Right away, there was an uproar. I threw myself right into it. I cried, and I protested that it wasn't my fault—it had just happened. She sighed, "You'll make us old before our time." My father butted in: "Those are new glasses that she hasn't even had for a month. It's like she does it on purpose. She doesn't know the value of things. Do you think money grows on trees?" They were even angrier about the fact that we would have to go back to the eye doctor. I was actually relieved that they were yelling at me. It cleansed me. I shed all the tears I had in me. It's true that my parents are sometimes a bit tight on funds at the end of the month, what with the bills, and now I had gone and screwed up these brand-new glasses. But they had already stopped talking about the glasses. "She has everything she needs to make her happy. No one could say we don't take care of her. Damn it! And I still have to talk to the teachers about all the books she's going to need for school." That seemed pretty far removed from the glasses, so I didn't answer. I had worse things weighing on me. My father said: "We'll get reimbursed. We just have to find the prescription. We might not even have to go back to the eye doctor." They had found a solution. But my mother refused to patch things up so quickly. My father was calmer. He must have been thinking about the banged-up car, the fact that it was his fault, which allied him with me. "You must not have been wearing your glasses," my mother went on. "You're trying to make trouble for us, young lady. Who are you trying to look good for, huh?" I was afraid she'd found out everything. I was never able to hide anything from her completely. That's what it is to be a parent: they spy on you when you're asleep, when you're eating, and when you're washing your . . . But she didn't know much. She just had a vague feeling. "Your friend, the beautiful Gabrielle—she's been giving you ideas. I saw her with a funny-looking guy with long hair." My father was bothered by this, looking a bit stunned. "She knows she's only supposed to be thinking about her studies. Isn't that right, Anne?" He was almost begging me, saying, "Come on now—be nice. Don't run around. Let's not have any scandals." Before, I used to play with him, and we would sing together: "A little hen on a wall, pecking on some stale bread, honey-fly, poopy-fly, what-a-fly." How far away that seemed. It seemed to me that my mother was starting to look like my grandmother. Her legs were swollen. In thirty years she would die, and I would be the age she is now—an atrocious cycle. I was suffocating. She went on, "We can't have more than one iron in the fire. Starting today, I'm going to keep an eye on you. There'll be no more of that." You can't answer someone when you feel so far away from them. Beating your own mother is the worst of all crimes. When I was six, I closed my eyes in horror, sure that if I imagined something the thing itself would happen. Now I would have liked her to be gone, dead, since in my mind I had already left her behind. I set my glasses down on the table. It was the first time I had the courage to walk out during an argument. Before, I would always stay glued to my chair while they said what I was like, how bad I was, and all the rest. In my bedroom, I cried some more. Do adults cry? That must be their "vale of tears." I was crying because they were yelling at me about a cracked lens in my glasses. What a waste that is when it's all the other things in your life that are going wrong. I got undressed. I stayed in front of the mirror, looking at myself. I heard them in the next room, with their usual puttering, setting the alarm clock, and the sound of them flushing the toilet. I didn't dare to touch myself. Mathieu had said, "That's mine now," and I always thought about that. It was as if what happened afterward, the shame of it, couldn't have been real. It's incredible how much we believe the things people tell us. It had only been a misunderstanding, or at least I tried to think about it that way, because it was too horrible to come home and realize that I had really messed things up for myself.

I turned the radio on very quietly, and again it was "J'attendrai le jour et la nuit." It was a syrupy song, but I liked it. I saw myself in the mirror, looking tan, with that black spot in the middle. I heard my parents sleeping, or at least my mother. My father yelled out, "Can't you turn off your radio? Are you trying to keep us up?" I have a body like hers, and I had to do what they did. "I'm telling you to turn off your light and go to sleep." Wouldn't anything be better than that, than those words? The next day I decided to go find Mathieu again and talk to him outside of the summer camp. I wanted to make love again for real, with the same trust we had before. Maybe it was crazy, but it seemed like true love, at least as far as I was concerned. I waited for him, he came, and then there was the breakup, like in a beautiful poem. I used to listen to a lot of records, and they always talked about how bad it feels, how you miss someone. They don't use the same words, so it never seems like they really mess things up the way I had. "Don't tell me you've never fiddled around with another girl. Listen, if you're going to get laid, you can't get hung up on feelings." I went into town wearing my old pair of glasses. I looked for errands to run. I bought some pens and notebooks for the start of the school year. I was walking on streets where I could have run into him at certain times of day, like at the café where he buys his cigarettes and his newspaper. I did that for three days in a row, and I really didn't know what I was looking for. At times I wasn't sure I had really slept with him. I repeated to myself in English—*To lie, to lie*—which means lying. They already had school satchels and sweaters in the shop windows, even though it was still very hot and dry. I stopped in front of every jumble of motorcycles, my legs heavy from the heat. I saw one that looked like his, but I was always getting it wrong, and I had to go back quickly so that I wouldn't make my mother suspect anything, especially on days when she wasn't working. It would have been better if she still worked in a factory, so that I could have some peace. Staying at home to take care of children is not always such a good thing. It depends on which side of it you're on. For me, in the end, it was a drag, because there were definitely times in the day when I would have been sure to run into him—around six in the evening—and instead I had to be at home. I watched my mother getting all worked up, ironing and smoothing out the laundry with her rough hand, always fussing around, making sure that everything was clean. What would people say about us if the curtains were to turn gray?! We had to hold onto our small share of pride. I think it was at the end of August that I completely stopped loving her, as the Point du Jour summer camp was about to end and the counselors were getting ready to leave. And I was going to stay. I would be going to school soon, and everything had been messed up. The only thing I would remember about the summer would be the yellow sink in the bathroom, the humiliation of it. My mother's hands were covered in red spots, her fingernails cut short. When she leaned down to the tile floor to wipe up spills, her legs widened and pushed against her gray skirt, and I could see the imprint of her girdle. She had no shape. I felt that I had left her behind. She's just an ordinary woman who always has the same conversations and always uses the same words. It's hard to think that I once adored her, or at least the kid who was me did. How unbelievable. I remember her voice, on the days when we had big family dinners. I would go to sleep, lying against her chest, and hear the words forming there. There was a rumble, as if I was being born out of that voice. It would have been fine with me if they had all died—even my father—but not her. At the seaside, I used to faint with horror when she would lean out into the void beyond the cliffs. I thought that she was going to let herself fall just to punish me for my badness, or to show me that she didn't need me. And she had the right to make me die if I was too naughty. "Don't touch yourself there, and never show it to anyone, you understand?" Except to her. She washed it and clothed it in fresh underpants. That was her sense of cleanliness. When Alberte started teaching me things, I was afraid that my mother would let me die, and that I would never know the years of getting my period, of having breasts that grew bigger, of having boys chase me. My body had gotten away from her without her even realizing it. She might get sick. That would be a way of slipping through her fingers and being able to get out onto the street. She had put me in a cocoon, wrapped me up in her skirt. I had dressed up in her clothes, smelling her odor of the kitchen and of powders, and her panties, with dried patterns on them that had gotten there somehow and that smelled like the inside of a cat's mouth. I always wanted to sleep in her bed with her. "Do you need to pee? You shouldn't hold it in: that's bad." I had thought that it was naughty to hold it in, a sin, because of the place where it came from, with its humid pleasures. But she never talked about pleasure. Urine was the only thing we could talk about. For three days, at six o'clock, I spun my heels in the house. He must have been in town. He always parked his motorcycle and went into the Commerce Café, and then he came back out and put his newspaper inside his shirt. I could have killed him. You always have to be wary of boys, of men—maybe even of my father. "Hey, close the bath-room door. Say, you old goat, you lech, can't you see there's someone in here. I'll go get the police if you keep doing it." The only major fault that she can never forgive me for is that I have pleasure. Luckily, there was Alberte. But it was never enough. Afterward, I would hang around her, asking her to tell me secrets about red and black things like the women's pussies and men's cocks painted on the old bridge with words of explanation written next to them. I wanted her to free me from that heavy weight, from the fact that all I thought about was "it," and that it suffocated me to have to think about it all by myself. I checked the time: it was six thirty. It would be over by now. Since my mother had never told me anything, when we started to have conversations, later on, I would act like I was interested in "it." That was cruel of me. Girls don't have the right to talk about it. There has to be a moral cleanliness. Just yesterday she was going on about it again. "Mrs. Buron, I always say that it has nothing to do with being rich, fortunately." I think that's why I can't love her anymore. She never explains the world to me in the way that I experience it, either in myself or in what is around me. She seems to be repeating things. When did she start trying to protect me with her stories about work, about morality, about doing what you're supposed to do? Maybe I didn't notice it before because when I was little I didn't pay attention to the words: childhood memories are a silent movie. Maybe if there hadn't been Mathieu, I would never have realized it so completely. She would have just been annoying to me. Now it was too late.

On August 30, at around five thirty, I went out. My shoes weren't going to be ready until that time. "You can go tomorrow." "No, I want to wear them tomorrow." She made a big hoopla about that. "You could wear the other pair." "They don't go with my dress." "Oh, aren't *you* fussy." "At least if I want to wear them I'll have them." "Fine, do what you want." I could finally get moving. My longest conversations with her always have a hidden agenda. If they didn't, what would be the point, just for a pair of shoes? In front of the Commerce, I saw his motorcycle. This time I was sure. I went into the shopping arcade across the street. The shop windows were a mirror for the whole street, with a bluish reflection like in a dream. But the women booksellers turned their heads to stare at me, and I looked at my watch as if I was waiting for someone and wondering, "What could he be doing?" He came out, the newspaper in his hand along with his helmet. He got on his motorcycle and stayed sitting there with his feet on the ground while he buckled his helmet. With his back a bit rounded, he lowered the visor and did a half-turn in my direction without starting his motorcycle. I was right at the entrance of the arcade. He started his motorcycle. He was probably just looking straight ahead, but I couldn't tell because of his helmet. He didn't seem to have seen me. On my way home, I opened my mouth wide and held my head slightly back. It's a thing I do to stop the tears from flowing. Otherwise, I would have looked like a crazy person walking along the street. That scares me, because I'm not always sure of *not* being crazy.

I really felt that way in September, after my father went back to work. He said, "I shouldn't be saying this, but you get bored by the end of summer vacation." It was true. The day after the day when I saw Mathieu for the last time, I stayed in front of the television set. My father was reading his newspaper, and some wasps were getting all worked up in the curtains. He smashed them with his newspaper and then burned them with his lighter. Things had started to go back to the way they were before I set foot in the Point du Jour camp. In the morning, setting a pile of sheets and blankets on the windowsill, my mother dusted until everything was spotless. I killed time in front of my café au lait. I ate another piece of toast, and then another, with lots of butter. The only thing I could think about was the taste of it in my mouth. My mother might have been happy to see me in the morning, even if I barely said hello to her. "Did you sleep well? There was a storm." "I didn't hear it." She knew that I would be going to high school soon, and she didn't care about anything else. Because she had been a factory worker. I looked around me, and it started to look like a stranger's house. I told myself that I would see Mathieu again, that he would write to me. He didn't have my address, but he could get it from Gabrielle, because Gabrielle would have given hers to Ratty, and he knew Ratty. Or else he would come back to the Point du Jour next year. There would be a year of homework assignments and of new people to meet in high school. An abyss. In two years, when I came of age, I would go to Paris and I would find him at whatever university he was going to. There was only one time I thought about leaving home right away and getting a job. But thinking about the train station, the platform, the crowd, and who knows what else, I got scared, seeing myself with my little suitcase in my hand. I always think of myself that way. When I think about my cousin Daniel, the hothead, I feel like the world doesn't belong to us, like we're afraid of it. My mother hung her linens outside. "What beautiful weather for drying the laundry." So did the neighbor woman. You can't just leave home. Secretly, I bought the same newspapers as Mathieu, so that I could at least keep up with his ideas, but it was too difficult. It was so far away from what our lives are like here. I don't read anymore. I don't read library books, or even go to the library. I'm not sure why. It would really have to be my story, and since it's not a story, there's not a huge chance that I would read it. I saw a book on the magazine kiosk: *Lost Illusions*. I leafed through it. It's illegible. They must not be the same illusions as mine. Afterward, I tried reading a magazine for girls of the "tender age," as they call it. There were letters from dozens of girls who had been dumped after sleeping with a boy. I wondered why people bother sending their stories to this woman. You know in advance what kind of reply they'll get: "Dear Jane: forget about so-and-so." But that's not the kind of answer I'm looking for. I want someone to explain to me why everything since July has happened, why I can't stand anything anymore, and how to go on living. Those things can't be found in a lonely-hearts letter. One girl was whimpering that she was pregnant, which was horrible and everything. "Confide in your mother," the lady answered, without cracking a smile. What a joke! I could see myself being in that girl's situation. I'm happy that I escaped disaster. That couldn't happen to me anymore, as I discovered one morning. With the blood, something else went out of me. There was nothing left of Mathieu: he was cleaned out, chased away by my own insides. It was sad. My periods usually measure time better than a calendar. So many things had happened between the last two periods. I remembered a secret horoscope that Alberte had scribbled out for me. "On the first day of your period, you look at it. If it's a really good one, that's a prediction." The number of days late it is also tells you something about the future. On Friday, I had written "sadness," and then on September 3, "two days late, more sadness." It wasn't very illuminating, and it was actually a bit depressing. I cleaned up my room and got my clothes ready for the start of the school year. I had started really eating a lot, munching on cookies and dried sausage all day long. And then, finally, I got my flow. When I went out into the yard to hang up the wet laundry, the lech neighbor was still there, his face twisted with perversity. It didn't matter to me now. He could crawl on the ground like a worm for all I cared. I said good morning. My mother told me to make a list of the clothes I needed. No more than four hundred francs, and not things that would look totally ridiculous on me. You can't be throwing money out the window. She was astonished that I had "noticed" my period so much this time. I had always known that she secretly pawed my dirty clothes and looked for evidence in the garbage bin. I bled for eight days, and whenever she was alone with me she asked me about it. "It's funny. You don't seem sick at all." It annoyed me that she wanted to talk about it. My periods were the tip of the iceberg, the one thing that she and I could talk about. But that could get dangerous if they ever stopped coming. On the Saturday before the start of the school year, my parents went to the supermarket. The car had been repaired. They came back with the trunk full. My mother had cleaned the interior of the car, and my father had washed the exterior. Everything was starting up again: the Saturday bounty, the thorough house cleaning, and the cowboy movies and songs on TV. As I watched my parents, I suddenly felt afraid that I was crazy. I took the cat into my room with me. She was enormous now. My father said she was going to have her little ones soon, but she should have already had them by then. I also think that I was jittery about the start of school. My brain wasn't ready to think about it yet.

Luckily, my glasses were repaired in time for me to wear them for the first day of school. The only person I recognized in my class was Céline. The parade of perky teachers always stunned me at the beginning of the school year. After that summer, seeing all of us sitting at tables in rows just like in elementary school made me feel like an outsider. I've never been comfortable with teachers: I'm wary of even the nicest ones. On the first day of school, you can still make yourself look minuscule. The teachers' eyes float around the room, looking at everyone. There were already students who were trying to get the teachers to pay attention to them by making intelligent remarks. They also gave us our class schedules. I didn't feel anything special when I saw that I had Thursday mornings free. It was sunny, and I looked out the windows, but not for long, since all I saw was red walls and other windows. You had to get to know all these new kids, especially the girls who were in literature classes with you. There's no rush to get to know the guys. There are two or three who aren't bad looking, but I can't see myself being with any of them—they seem like yokels to me. Add to the mix that the boys always pretend not to be interested in the girls who are in their grade. In the breaks, a lot of them are talking about their summer vacations. I felt that Céline would soon latch onto some friends other than me. The two of us aren't alike enough. She had spent a month in Yugoslavia. I wondered how far she had gone with her flirting, her breasts tucked up neatly under her top. You never know with other people. The French teacher gave us an assignment for an essay that was due in three weeks, which seemed like the end of time to me. Before, I used to like the start of the school year: the disorder, the new faces, the change of scenery. On the first Wednesday after school started, I couldn't help myself: I went back to the Point du Jour. The camp was closed, and the little window was in the wrong place for me to be able to see inside. I walked along the edge of the lawn, and I saw the black poop from the dog that had been sick the first time we all talked together. That had been a month and a half ago. How much longer would it still be there? I was happy to be there. I hadn't thought I would ever need to go back. Pedaling home, I calculated that it had been two months since my grandmother died. Two months ago, she hadn't suspected anything was wrong with her. I imagined her reading the little newspapers they lent her, and *Pilgrimage Magazine*. Up in her attic, there were bunches of dried beans hanging upside down from the ceiling. They crackled when I walked under them. But she was old.

I ran into one of the guys who had been riding their motor scooters last July, Gabrielle's friends. He didn't know whether to stop or not. He circled around a few times, and I waited for him at the edge of the sidewalk. I wanted to see someone from the time before Mathieu, from before the summer camp and everything. Basically, I wanted to see if there had been any sign of what was to come. It was as if now that I had the whole summer behind me, I could start over. His name was Michel, and he was eighteen. What he lacked was mostly conversational skills. Since he worked in a garage, we didn't have many subjects in common that would have allowed me to prolong the small talk and make me forget the goal. Boy-girl friendship is either a bluff, or else it's what happens later. As it turned out, we made a rendezvous for Thursday morning. He would figure out an explanation for missing work. I'd figure one out too, because when I want to deceive my parents I can always do it, though it's tiring. Looking at his pasty white cheeks, I wondered if it was even worth it. Maybe just for the sake of continuing my streak. When I woke up on Thursday, the thought of meeting him felt like a burden. I like staying in bed, feeling the cold sheets against my face, with it all warm inside, my nightie climbing up to my waist. To remind myself what it felt like, I spread my legs, but just thinking about it made me want to cry. He was on the street next to the school, pretty far away from the entrance. It wasn't going to happen with the guys in high school. Ha ha. He bumped my leg with his scooter as a joke, and afterward he kept jumping up and down on the seat, lifting up a wheel every so often. It was annoying, because he looked at me in a weird way, as if I had been staring at his jeans on the seat of the scooter. I was clear about what I was doing. We went into a bistro, and he played pinball. I watched his hips moving toward the machine and the blinking lights. He sprawled out next to me and started going through my canvas bag. He took out my glasses, and I cried out. I would make do with my broken pair from now on rather than risk getting sent to juvenile hall. Then he took out my schoolbooks. He leafed through them, making faces. Then he suddenly got sad and closed his eyes, saying, "You can't imagine how much everything sucks for me." I asked him why, even though I was too sick of everything myself to be able to take care of him as well. It all came out: it was his parents and his job. He repeated, "Everything sucks." Maybe we did have things in common after all. But his language soon petered out. I asked him if he was interested in politics. "Which newspapers do you read?" "Oh, you're not going to bore me with all that stuff, are you?" He didn't like it when I talked to him about things he didn't know about. I repeated what Mathieu had explained to me, but he didn't know anything about it. I've noticed that boys don't like it when you try to educate them. I had already checked out some buildings that were under construction, in case they could prove useful. It was pretty chilly out. In the evenings, my father was grumbling that my mother had cold feet and that she shouldn't come too close to him. That was a sign that fall was coming, and colder weather. I had my big sweater on, and a smaller one underneath, and my velour jeans. I didn't know what to say to him. "You know, the first time we saw each other, when I was with Gabrielle? My grandmother died two weeks later." He seemed stunned. I didn't know if he was thinking about her or about nothing. Then, suddenly, he said, "Oh, really?" I was always running late, and this day was no different. There was just one hour left. He breathed heavily, which I didn't like. He didn't say anything either dirty or nice, but he seemed content and sweet. Parents think it's just about going with anyone. I didn't even know his last name, only the name of the garage where he worked. I thought that maybe it was because I was wearing so many clothes, but I didn't feel anything. I could feel his cold hands on the nape of my neck, and it was very draughty in the room under construction that we had gone into. He put his hands under my big sweater, and it still felt the same way. I wanted to take his hands out. What mainly disgusted me was that his eyes were closed. I felt "it"—his sex, I mean. The general term would fit this time. It all made me a bit sick to my stomach. I thought about the empty space inside me, and it was as if it had closed itself off from far away, from the top of my stomach. I was wearing the same jeans I had been wearing the last time at the summer camp. I thought about the letters from the "young girls of a tender age": "What should you do if you don't want to do anything?" "Well, you say you don't want it, but all the girls do it. If you were a nurse . . ." I was feeling more and more disgusted by him, and I pulled away from him. "I have to go home. My mother will ask questions." He was really flustered, but I didn't care. I think what I felt was the opposite of caring. I pulled my sweater back down and fixed my hair. Touching without pleasure, that's the solution. Well, here it was. We went back out, holding hands until we got to the road. Since I didn't want to see him again, I thought we could at least part on good terms. I took out my secret little notebook, and I wrote the name "Michel" under "Yan" and "Mathieu," with the date, Thursday, September 22. That Saturday, when I got home from school, my mother said, "Did you see in the paper who's getting married? Alberte Retout, the girl you used to play with when we lived on Rue Césarine." Actually, she had already gotten married: you could see her in the photo wearing a long dress, hardly recognizable. "Did you see who she picked?" my father asked. "A young man who works for the railroad. But it looks like she's pretty well set up with her office job." They seemed satisfied, as they always do when everything is going smoothly, as if nothing could be different from what it was and everything was in order. I felt terribly blue seeing Alberte, yet another girl I didn't want to be like. But we used to have fun together, seeing who could play dead in the grass for longer, our four legs up in the air, and then, "Hey, will you show me your pads when they're full of blood?" And she was no phony: she kept her word. That day when the old lech was there, the neighbor, we weren't expecting it. We had only been living in the new house for a week. Maybe that's why he thought he could get away with it. These sadists are full of delusions. Right in front of us in the middle of his yard. "We're not scared of you," Alberte said. She was very smart. I thought he might have been holding a camera. He had his hands in his pockets, and he was pulling on his trouser legs. She yelled out, "I'm going to report you to the police. Come on, Anne. It's not worth putting on your glasses for." Alberte, who wanted to be a stewardess. She used to say, "I'll call myself Cendra." My parents were going on about it while we were eating the salad. "To tell the truth, she wasn't so good in school, but she didn't do too badly for herself. She'll make a pretty good living as a secretary, with her husband working for the railroad." Was it even the same Alberte? She used to joke, "When I have children, I'm going to put them down the toilet hole." If this was still her, what had made her change? My father shouted at me: "And what about you? Don't you have anything to say about it? You haven't said a word all through dinner." In class, I was having a harder and harder time concentrating. At first, I thought all the schoolwork was easy. It was things that were a review of what we had done the year before, and I had been a good student before the summer. I got a bad grade in math. Fortunately, my parents wouldn't learn about it until the end of the trimester. In physics, I watched the teacher, who was so cold and intelligent, while I was so heavy, with my thighs stuck to the bottom of the table. I was a real fatso. There's a fairy tale where some guys offer to sell meters' worth of fabric to a king, and no one can see the color of the damn cloth, but everyone pretends to admire it anyway. I was like those bumpkins in the old days, but it was actually worse because I thought I was the only one who didn't see anything underneath when I undressed the teacher. Watching Céline and the others, I wondered who was pushing them so hard, why they wanted to ask so many questions. Either they cheat, or they ask to do an oral report. "On such and such a day?" "Yes, ma'am." I took notes, because they notice if you don't, but when I reread them, they were just hieroglyphs. "Is school getting too hard for you?" they always ask in my family. "You have to be really smart to keep up." I was astonished to be the first one in the family to make it this far. I had thought I would end up doing the technical exam like Alberte. For a long time, I thought I couldn't be as intelligent as Céline because of my modest background. I had been right, and here was the proof. Things had started off badly in terms of becoming a schoolteacher. At first, I had wanted to be a social worker. I told my parents, and my mother replied that it was not suitable for me, going into slums, with all kinds of people, and foreigners. "I just can't see you doing that." At eight o'clock, in class, I look at myself as if nothing had happened, as if there were no differences between us, except for intelligence, that little invisible flame. There are no bodies in class, and yet mine was coming at me from every side. I walked home from school with Céline, and we talked, vaguely, with our eyes looking straight ahead at the road. Before, she hadn't been a better student than me, but she was always very put-together, like a very slow, very brown block. She probably doesn't have any problems at home. Her apartment must be like the inside of the eye doctor's office: huge, sunny, and magnificent. I wondered if her parents gave her the same claptrap as mine did about studying, and about her behavior and everything. I asked her about it. Yes, of course they wanted Céline to get her *bac* so that she could go on to university afterward. But that seemed so obvious to them that they didn't bug her as much as mine did. What makes my parents so annoying is that they're afraid I'm not going to succeed. I was discovering that I was less and less able to stand Céline. Walking next to her, I suddenly felt that I was superior to her—something I never would have thought before the summer—because I knew about so many things that she obviously didn't know about, like my parents' lousy jobs, the tight ends of months, and vacations where we don't go anywhere. But maybe that's not really a form of superiority, since I didn't dare to tell Céline about it.

The only thing left to tell is what started happening at the beginning of October. Seeing my menstrual blood was something that always made me happy. We don't have to get in fights like boys to make our blood flow—calmly and without violence—every month. But this time it was late. One Sunday, when it was very hot, we went to Aunt Elise's house. She asked my father, "When are you going to get your daughter married off?" My mother said, "She has plenty of time. Her studies come first. We don't want to have more than one iron in the fire." I smiled graciously during their conversation. Just because I didn't like my mother anymore didn't mean I had to cause trouble for her in front of everyone or tell them they didn't know what they were talking about. They were smiling, happy that the order of irons in the fire had been respected so far. And it was right after that, while eating the main course, that they starting talking about Monique, my aunt who was still just as stupid as ever, and about Daniel. "It's fine to brag about how brave you are, but you still have to find work, and he's a hothead." I had the feeling that I wouldn't get it this month, or maybe even in the months to come. That it had just stopped for no reason. They were all arguing, and my brain was getting chopped into little pieces by their words. It felt like there was a big shadow falling over me, like on those evenings when we used to play at the house on Rue Césarine. Space seemed to shrink until it was no bigger than the bottom of one of the glasses on the table. It didn't matter if I didn't get my periods anymore. My aunt said, "Cat got your tongue, Anne? You used to be more talkative." It was more like *their* tongues that I had lost track of. Everything felt jumbled up inside me, and it didn't line up with what they were saying. With Mathieu, it still did, or it seemed like that to me, but it's better not to think about him, or I'm afraid I'll go crazy. That evening, my mother criticized me for eating too much. "What are people going to think of you? You should always leave the table feeling hungry." We ate supper at home. She gathered the crumbs from her bread together and threw them onto the middle of her plate, which she had wiped clean. My father was already watching his movie. "Say," she asked, "have you 'noticed' anything yet this month?" "Well, no." "What could have happened to throw you off your cycle?" Every day after that she asked me again, with a smile but no kind word. When my father was around, she changed the subject. She must not love him anymore either.

I knew she would drag me to see Berdouillette the following Saturday. She couldn't think about anything else. I wasn't afraid of anything, although there was always a little doubt in my mind. Alberte and I always told each other unbelievable things, like that you could have a baby just from touching someone. And in the magazines, it said being pregnant didn't necessarily stop your period. In the waiting room, she didn't read any of the magazines that were spread out on the table. It was cold in Dr. Louvel's office, and it wasn't very luxurious. There was just one carved chest that was a bit showoffy. She seemed to think it was expensive. We only like to have new things in our house. She had her legs pulled under her, and her hands were resting on her handbag just like at the eye doctor's. This was, of course, yet another thing we were doing for my benefit, so that everything could go back to the way it was before, with a sense of order. Maybe she also thought of it as finding harmony: not for herself, the poor thing, but for me. I suddenly had an image of her: it was at Veules-les-Roses, with Aunt Monique and Daniel. I was seven, and my mother was wearing a dress with red flowers on it. She laughed out loud, and we fished mussels out of piles of sand. She laughed so hard that she had to wash her underwear in the ocean, because of the pee. At a café near the beach, they drank aperitifs, and we ate cakes—*religieuses* that Daniel had gotten from the bakery next door. The two of them were bent in two with laughter, and the aperitifs flashed in the sun. That image of her was so far removed from the words and the principles that she had now: of not being noticed, of being bolted down, of not being rich but still living in the way you were expected to. What does she know about people with money, other than their houses seen from the outside and their living rooms on TV? Or the rich girls who go by our house on Sunday on their horses, with their butts going up and down, not looking at anyone from under their stupid-looking helmets. Céline rides horses. It's only the things that *aren't* allowed us that make me know things she doesn't. Maybe it's the same way in all families that aren't rich. And the mothers are even worse. I would have liked my mother to still be that infinite weight of flesh in a red dress, who laughed and who let me do whatever I wanted that day. Louvel opened the door. He was all bouncy at first, but he got serious when my mother told him what had happened to me. He glued his pink head to my chest, and then he pressed on my stomach. My mother waited with confused eyes for the mystery to be solved beneath his fingers so that she would finally know why things weren't working right anymore. Ever since I was born, he's told them everything about my body. I looked at his head, which seemed smaller than before. He twisted himself around in his chair to examine me. Even so, I was sure he wouldn't find anything. I would have fooled both of them. Even if he could tell her the only thing that really interested her—is she still a virgin?—she would never have been able to say, "It's all right for you to check." It was up to him to deal with it, as he made her understand with his fixed eyes. He was cautious: maybe he didn't want a scandal. "It's just a simple amenorrhea, my dear lady, very common in young girls. A few pills, and everything will be back in order." She didn't understand the word very well. He translated it, but she didn't seem very relieved. "But what caused it, doctor?" "Worries, studies. It's the age when they fret, you know." He was playing it smart, talking about the anxiety attacks that adolescent girls get, which are the same for everyone. I would have preferred it if he hadn't explained anything about me to my mother. But she would definitely believe him. She paid the money a bit less quickly than she had at the eye doctor's. I had the feeling that she was bewildered in spite of his explanation, that there was something about my condition she still didn't get. "If we need to," she said when we had gone out the door, "we can go see a specialist. I'm not going to leave you like this. We have to get you back to normal. We're not going to tell your father about it: he would worry." Only the doctor and her would know. We didn't say a word to each other the rest of the way home.

I've already taken one bottle of the pills, with no effect. Things are going less and less well in school. At home, I criticized the physics teacher, and my parents wouldn't stand for it. "Your teacher knows a lot more about it than you do." So I prefer to go back to my room and reread books, just for show. All that stuff doesn't interest me anymore. The neighbor woman doesn't hang up her clothes to dry as often now because it's too cold. I like to stay in town after my classes, which is only possible when my mother is at the Petite Vitesse. I'm always seeing guys who look like Mathieu, blond with long hair and a motorcycle. I run toward them, they turn around, and I stop. If they at least knew that it was because they looked like him, we might get along. I would go with them just because they look like him. But that's not the feeling I get from them. They think I'm running after them. I thought about a book we read in ninth grade. It's called *Le Grand Meaulnes*, and it's about a guy who was searching for something. But in books it's always the boys who are walking around with their noses to the wind. Is there a *la grande meal-nesse*? I didn't like that book. I don't want to see Michel again. I like to smoke, but the problem is finding money for cigarettes. I asked for more for my allowance. My father answered, "Where does it all go? You really need to earn your own living so that you realize the value of things." It would be better if they taught us that earlier. It would be more useful that way. It's when I'm in class that the world seems shiniest, the most distant. I'm beginning to wonder if I actually had that summer vacation, if I really slept with Mathieu, and then a bit with Yan and Michel. The difference between whether I did or didn't seems tiny, maybe because I'm in tenth grade as was planned all along, and the teacher is asking for the next homework assignment in a week's time, and it's the same date for everyone. It makes you lose touch with reality when everything seems to be standing still around you. I would rather be crazy for real. They would take care of me, I could sleep all day, they would bring me food on a platter, there would be beautiful mountains like in the photos of sanatoriums, I could listen to records, and I wouldn't have to move anymore. Or else there could be Mathieu's revolution: not for stealing things, but for the fancy bedrooms, the big beds, and the trips. The fact that I was poor would turn out to be essential for surviving in nature, like in the books I read when I was a little kid where the parents were erased after the first few pages. I can understand that. They're the ones who tire you out, and it's even on their account that I won't have the courage to leave, and that I'll try not to go crazy. Until the age of five, I believed that people *bought* their children. Actually, when you think about it, that would have been easier. Your whole childhood and adolescence would be temporary, just waiting for them to get paid back for what they spent. In real life, you're stuck with them. Maybe Mathieu got it wrong. The place you start from isn't your social condition—it's your parents.

The cat slept on my parents' unmade bed one morning, with her stomach swollen like it was going to explode. She wasn't licking herself anymore, and she wasn't drinking. When I came home from school, my mother told me right away that she had died. I wanted to see her, but she had already buried her in the yard. "What did you expect? She had a good long life. It's just like with people." I had a desperate desire to cry, which it hurt me to do in front of my mother. I remembered how last March the cat was still rolling around on patches of upturned dirt while I studied math. That was far away now. My mother said she had put the cat on my pillow in my bedroom so that she could make the bed—naturally, you couldn't leave the bed unmade all day long—and she died afterward. The pillowcase would have to be changed: it had a stain on it that was pinkish on the edge and yellow in the middle. She must have licked herself just before she died. Piss and blood are the last memories I'll have of her. The cat had to die one day or another, and I had to go on living. My grandmother also had to die. I remembered the warm, black kittens that my father had buried in the garden, while the cat was mewling, locked inside the house. I dug them up one day, when we were living on Rue Césarine. They were all caked with earth. I was happy for five minutes, and then my father came out. He slapped me so hard that I was bowled over and dropped the kittens. He picked them up as if they were cabbage cores, then reinforced the ground over them by stamping on it with his foot. Their eyes would never open again. My parents were furious with me that whole evening, telling me I was crazy. "I'll get the teacher to punish you, you'll see." I didn't understand about death yet. They've gone to the supermarket together, their weekly outing, with boxes prepared for the groceries, their checkbook, and their spotless car. I have more than two hours to work on my essay. The October fair has started, the one for the festival of Saint Luke. What would I even do there if I went, since guys like Michel are a dime a dozen around the bumper cars? Yesterday my mother told me, "I'm really tempted not to let you go to the fair or the movies until you start getting normal periods again." She blushed, as if something had gotten away from her, as if she was having strange thoughts. I spread out *France-Soir* on the living room table to protect the varnish. It's too cold in my room, what with the rain. I have nothing to say about the topic the teacher gave us, just disordered thoughts. If I let myself go, if I was free to write about whatever I wanted, I would write about blood and cries, and there would be a red dress too, and jeans. People don't suspect the importance of clothes in what happens to us. And there would be meals in the kitchen. My father would say something he had heard some-where, and my mother would stretch out a tired leg. I would write about anything, as long as it made a tight knot around me. But it wouldn't make sense. I would get lost in the details, like my parents do when they go in circles while telling their stories and can't find a way out. At lunch, my father told us that Daniel had gotten arrested while he was leaving a dance. Once again there had been a fight. He'll never do anything right. Even so, they seemed sad as they ate. Will I turn out like him if I do badly in high school? I'm afraid of everything now. It's something very vague, a dark cloud inside my heart. I'll never finish my essay, and the teacher will give me a zero. She's the one who says, when the mood takes her, "You can change your life—you have to change your life." So what is she still doing here?

October 1976

CPSIA information can be obtained
at www.ICGtesting.com
Printed in the USA
LVHW111922111022
730461LV00004B/775